"You said I was safe.
You said you'd protect me."

"I did. You made it safely home, didn't you?" His words were short but not unkind.

"I made it home, anyway."

Those blue eyes sliced into hers.

"What does that mean?"

"Someone has been following me, and I think it's the same man from Lybania."

His arms crossed over his broad chest, the sleeves of his T-shirt pulling snug around his biceps. He looked so intimidating.

"Did you call the police? Tell them you're being stalked, and they can look into it for you. They can handle things like that."

"They wouldn't help me." If she had any idea how to face down the man following her on her own, she would. But since she didn't, she had to convince the lieutenant to help.

Taking a firm step toward him, she pointed her finger toward his chest. "Listen to me. I'm in trouble, but it's not just me. I don't know the name of the man who's after me, but I know what I heard. He's plotting to blow something up...here in San Diego."

Books by Liz Johnson

Love Inspired Suspense

The Kidnapping of Kenzie Thorn
Vanishing Act
Code of Justice
*A Promise to Protect
*SEAL Under Siege

*Men of Valor

LIZ JOHNSON

After graduating from Northern Arizona University in Flagstaff with a degree in public relations, Liz Johnson set out to work in the Christian publishing industry, which was her lifelong dream. In 2006 she got her wish when she accepted a publicity position with a major trade book publisher. While working as a publicist in the industry, she decided to pursue her other dream—becoming an author. Along the way to having her novels published, she wrote articles for several magazines and worked as a freelance editorial consultant.

Liz makes her home in Nashville, Tennessee, where she enjoys theater, exploring her new home and making frequent trips to Arizona to dote on her nephew and three nieces. She loves stories of true love with happy endings.

SEAL UNDER SIEGE

LIZ JOHNSON

HARLEQUIN® LOVE INSPIRED® SUSPENSE

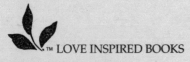 ™ LOVE INSPIRED BOOKS

ISBN-13: 978-0-373-44554-7

SEAL UNDER SIEGE

www.LoveInspiredBooks.com

Printed in U.S.A.

The Lord hath anointed me to preach good tidings unto the meek; he hath sent me to bind up the brokenhearted, to proclaim liberty to the captives, and the opening of the prison to them that are bound.
—Isaiah 61:1

For sweet friends who have encouraged me along this journey and fell for these SEALs right along with me.

Ashley Boyer, Staci Carmichael Havlik,
Jessica Barnes, Amy Haddock, Kaye Dacus,
Kristi Smith, and Katie Bond,
my life is richer for knowing you.

Thanks for the brainstorms,
book talk, and belly laughs.

ONE

Lt. Tristan Sawyer whispered into the mic that brushed the corner of his mouth. "Rock, are you in position?"

Night hung over him like a blanket, wrapping up all of his senses, except his hearing, as he waited for the sound of his senior chief's voice. "Affirmative."

Across the street Petty Officer Will Gumble lurked next to the window of a crumbling single-story home. The house—not even a mile from the Persian Gulf—had been cleaned out, probably weeks ago, and Willie G. had swept it again to make sure there wouldn't be any surprises when they moved in on their target.

He took two short breaths and lifted his night vision goggles, giving the street another check. It was deserted except for the five stonelike figures hidden along the street. He spotted them only because he knew they were there. He'd scouted and scoped each location in preparation for this moment. He'd studied the maps and floor plans, packed his gear and prepared his mind.

All for this moment.

His blood began to pump harder, picking up speed. He tightened, then loosened his grip on the weapon in his hand, forcing his breath into a steady rhythm and his heart into an even pattern.

He was ready. But he had to wait for the signal that their boats were nearly in place at the extraction point. If they moved too soon, they'd recover the "packages"—three American hostages—but have no place to deliver them. If they waited too long, they left the inflatable boats open to discovery.

Timing was everything, so he schooled his muscles, keeping them alert yet relaxed until the signal.

A double click came through his earpiece.

Time to rock and roll.

"Let's go." Just like they'd practiced, he swung around the back of the building where Senior Chief Matt Waterstone, also known as Rock, wrenched open a window on the basement level and slid into the darkness below. Tristan followed suit until his shoulder caught on the frame. He wiggled, his feet still not quite on the floor.

The team was on radio silence for this part of the mission, but he didn't need to see or hear his best friend to know Matt was laughing at him.

After what felt like an hour suspended by the snagged shoulder of his battle dress uniform, he reached across his body and yanked on it until it let go with a tear.

He dropped to his feet, squatting and squinting into the dark, his weapon at the ready. On the far side of the box of a room, the door cracked open and light filtered in. The weak sliver of a stream made it only halfway across the floor, but it did illuminate Matt's gloved hand on the edge of the door.

Tristan moved forward, staying low. They'd done this enough to know the drill. He would move first down the hallway, Matt positioned at his six—covering his blind spot. Back-to-back, they'd sweep the basement, looking for the packages. Intel said there were two women and a man.

They had been held here for at least three weeks, though word of their captivity had just reached the SEAL teams.

Only God knew what the three had endured. At least two of them were in their sixties. The people of Lybania tended to respect their elders. As for the girl in her twenties...

A shiver ran down his spine. He couldn't think about that. He had to get her free and secure first. Once they were all safely out of this pit and away from men who kidnapped aid workers for no reason, he'd let the ones trained to deal with her situation handle it.

For now, he'd do what he was trained to.

Matt motioned for them to stop, opening a door with the toe of his boot. He must have encountered less resistance than he expected, since it flung open like a piece of paper on hinges, flapping against the opposite wall.

Tristan shook his head at Matt, who shrugged a shoulder and offered a smirk by way of apology for the unnecessary noise. Luckily, the walls of the building could have been from the biblical era, all crumbling blocks that muffled errant doors and shuffling feet. Matt led the way into the room, clearing it before stepping back into the hallway.

With two fingers, Tristan pointed toward the stairwell at the end of the hall. Matt nodded, taking the rear as they climbed from the dimness of the basement into relative light. It wasn't much brighter than a full moon, but compared to the inky darkness below, the second floor radiated, removing any possibility of hiding in the shadows.

His earpiece clicked twice, and he swung his fingers in a quick barrel roll at Matt. They had fifteen minutes to get the American prisoners and get them to the extraction point on the gulf. No time to waste.

Matt nodded, held a hand to his ear and motioned to

the door on his left. At least two voices carried through the wall, their Arabic words getting louder.

"Cards," he mouthed. Apparently someone was cheating. If there was no honor among thieves, there was less among kidnapping terrorists.

Tristan motioned that they should pass the door without incident if possible. Their mission wasn't to take down this cell or alert anyone to their presence. Their only job was to snatch and go.

The door to the room with the card game stood open about three inches, so he held up his hand, waiting for another argument as a diversion. They didn't disappoint, tempers exploding like one of Matt's C-4 bricks. In the fray the two SEALs bolted down the hall, passing three closed doors on each side.

An empty chair sat outside the last door on the right, the guard most likely wrapped up in the card game they'd passed.

Tristan jiggled the handle of the door, but it stuck in place. In a flash Matt was there by his side, his lock-picking kit in hand.

Tristan had known Matt since the first day of Basic Underwater Demolition/SEAL training and in all that time, he had yet to see a lock his friend couldn't pick. Man, it was a good thing Matt was on the teams. He'd be dangerous on the wrong side of the law.

Tristan held his weapon at the ready, standing guard until the old lock popped and the door swung in. He backed into the room, letting Matt take the first sweep and shutting out most of the noise and light from the hall with the closed door.

The space was empty save for two figures huddled in the corner, hands clasped together. He held a finger to his lips as he squatted in front of the shadowed, grandfatherly man. "I'm with the United States Navy." He whispered the words, which seemed intent on filling the entire room. "Are you Judith and Hank Timmons?"

The man's gray hair bobbed into the shard of light coming from the hallway. "Yes." It seemed to take all his energy just to utter the single syllable, and he slumped against his wife.

Tristan offered them both a reassuring grin and gently squeezed the man's bony elbow. "We're going to get you out of here. But I need you to move quickly and quietly and do exactly what I say. Do you understand?"

The couple nodded in unison, their faces drawn and weary but their eyes alight with hope. For good reason.

"This is my teammate." He motioned to Matt's towering shadow. "Ma'am, this is the senior chief. He's going to help you up and out the window."

She shook her head, holding on to her husband's arm with both hands. "I won't leave him."

"He'll be right behind you."

Matt squatted down in front of the woman and held out his hand. "I promise you'll be okay. There are more of our team outside, waiting for you. You don't want to make them miss the boat out of here, do you?"

She frowned for a split second before Matt had her on her feet and shuffling toward the window. Mr. Timmons wasn't going to let his wife out of his sight, so he pushed himself off the dusty floor, following closely behind.

Tristan glanced over his shoulder toward the empty hallway before whispering into his mic, "Second story, northwest corner."

"Copy that." Then a short pause before Willie continued, "We see you."

As Matt slipped a harness around Mrs. Timmons, she

clutched at his flak vest, shaking him. "You have to help Staci. They took her last week."

"Do you know where they took her?"

Mrs. Timmons looked out the window she was about to be lowered through. "No."

"It'll be all right. Hang on tight and walk down the wall or you'll scrape against it. Got it?" Matt scooped the nodding woman into his arms, sliding her feet-first through the window, lowering her on the rope that slipped expertly through his hands.

The rope went slack for a moment, and then it was tugged twice, the signal from Willie G. that the package had arrived to them. Matt pulled it back up and immediately hooked it to a harness under Mr. Timmons's arms.

Tristan pressed his mic to his lip. "Second package on the way. The third has been moved. We'll search the rest of the building and meet you at the extraction point."

Willie clicked his mic twice—roger that—as Mr. Timmons slid through the window with a little help from Tristan and Matt.

Just as the rope went slack again, the door behind them cracked with the force of an angry kick. He and Matt both dove to the darkest parts of the room along opposite walls.

As he rolled, Tristan pulled his knife from his boot. Gunfire would draw unwanted attention from neighbors, which the team on the ground didn't need as they hustled two dehydrated, malnourished seniors down dark alleys.

The two new occupants swore loudly in Arabic as they ran into the room. They asked over and over where the old man and woman had gone, their words carrying down the hall where several more angry voices joined the fray.

Tristan caught Matt's eye across the room and didn't even have to signal. They knew what they were doing, knew what had to happen. Simultaneously, they each aimed for the man closest to them, quickly rendering each harmless with a blow to the neck.

His hand tingled as his Lybanian target—or "tango," as Tristan had been trained to call them—crumpled to the ground, and he wiggled his fingers. But there wasn't time to think about it more than that as five more men barreled into the room.

Letting his training and survival instincts take over, he spun to the left and dropped to the floor just as one of the men fired his semiautomatic into the wall. So much for avoiding gunfire. With a sweep of his leg, Tristan took the tango down at his ankles, even as his gun continued to discharge.

Caught by one of the stray bullets, another tango yelped and crashed into the wall, shaking the whole house, as though the ancient mud blocks were just waiting for an excuse to give way.

As he slumped to the floor, the tango yelled at one of the others to go kill the girl. The last to enter the room spun and ran back the way he had come.

"Be right back," Tristan yelled at Matt, who just grunted in response.

He charged down the narrow corridor toward the stairwell, praying he wouldn't be too late to save the last package.

Staci Hayes clutched a scrap of paper to her chest with both hands as the voices in the room below her rose to frantic cries, punctuated with the unmistakable sound of gunfire.

She sucked in a breath, fear making her shiver despite the heat that pushed her to the lowest point in the room.

Dear Lord, help Judy and Hank if that's where the guards are headed.

Something popped beneath her feet, and she scrambled into a corner, tucking her knees under her chin and staring into the impossible darkness. Always darkness.

A voice screamed a Lybanian curse, but his words were cut off in the middle of his rage. Something banged into one of the walls, shaking the whole house once again.

In the stillness that followed, she held herself together only by a string of prayers, her eyes still searching the thick darkness for any sign. Of what, she wasn't sure. This was clearly more than just another card game gone wrong. But what was causing such a struggle?

On shaking legs she pushed herself to stand, tucking the piece of paper beneath her collar and into the lining of her undershirt. She ran empty hands along the crumbling wall and turned the corner when she reached it. Silence still prevailed below as she reached the door, jiggling the locked handle for the hundredth time.

But this time when she pulled her hand back, it rattled again. Someone was out there.

Scurrying backward to her safe corner, she tripped on her floor-length robe and fell sprawled on her backside.

Just as she landed, the frame around the door splintered and the panel flew open. She threw her hands over her eyes, protecting them from the sudden glare of light added to her world, but not before she made out the silhouette of a man whose broad shoulders filled the empty frame.

He screamed at her in Arabic as he ran toward her corner, his words drowned out by the ringing in her ears.

And then there were two men, a second silhouette materializing behind the first. Her eyes were stinging from the light, blurring the images, but the second man pushed the first man, who crumpled to the ground.

It was a dream. It had to be. Or maybe her eyes without her contacts or glasses were playing tricks on her.

But no matter how hard she squinted, there were still two men, one on the ground and the other standing over him, looking gigantic and ominous with the backlighting casting his face in shadows. Breath catching in her throat and heart pounding painfully, she pulled her knees even closer, pressing her forehead against them and praying, not for the first time, that she had dreamed the whole ordeal.

She heard the second man cross the room and squat down at her side. "Are you Staci Hayes?" His words were so soft that she looked up to read his lips, but she couldn't miss her name there or the American accent she had only heard once in the previous week.

She nodded, but words failed her.

His white teeth flashed, and he pointed at himself. "I'm with the United States Navy. I'm here to get you safely back to the States." His ice-blue eyes flashed with a strength that expected to be obeyed.

She tried again to speak, but her tongue stuck to the roof of her mouth. He put his hand on her arm, gentle yet firm. "Ms. Hayes, I'm going to get you out of here, but I need you to do everything I say quickly and without question."

"What—what about Judy and Hank?"

"They're safe." He looked over his shoulder at the guard he'd taken down, who still lay motionless. "Can you run?"

"Yes." But the shaking in her knees threatened to make her a liar, and she rubbed her hands up and down her shins.

"We've got to rock and roll, L.T."

She jerked at the deep voice coming from the doorway, but before she could do more than that, he was by her other side, both men tugging her to her feet.

L.T. didn't waste time with introductions, instead asking his tall friend, "Did you take care of them?"

"Yes. But one got a call-off. Backup is on the way, I think."

"You think?" L.T.'s eyes flashed.

"Hey, I'm not the language expert on the team."

She'd been so wrapped up in their rapid back-and-forth that she barely noticed that they'd crossed the room and were propelling her toward the stairway.

"Stay with me and, whatever happens, don't let go of my hand." He held her hand up to her eyes and squeezed her fingers until she squeezed his back. "Got it?"

"Yes." She wrapped her other hand around his wrist as the two navy men sailed down the stairs. Her skirt whipped around her ankles and she stepped on the side of it, nearly sending her tumbling into L.T.'s back. She caught herself by the grip on his arm at the last minute, and he glanced over his shoulder at her, the look in his eyes asking if she was all right. She nodded quickly, and he spun around.

By the time they reached the front door of the building, she was breathing as if she'd climbed Mount Everest, her lungs screaming for air and heart pounding hard.

L.T. paused for a moment, looking down the midnight streets. She took the chance to gulp in deep breaths, sure that they'd be gone just as fast.

Without a word, the second man slipped into the night, his gun lifted to his shoulder in rock-steady hands. Staci and L.T. followed him into the cloak of darkness.

"Hang in there," he whispered just as a bullet burst in the sand at their feet.

Every thought vanished as her feet pounded the streets, winding between buildings and down alleys until her ragged breaths were louder than her footfalls. Sweat ran down her back and arms, but she refused to loosen her damp grip on L.T.'s hand, even as he tucked her into his side.

Another round flew past them, slamming into a building, as men began shouting at them to stop. "Got to pick it up." L.T. tugged on her hand, somehow pulling her forward and pushing from behind.

She gasped for a breath and swiped at the sweat rolling from her forehead into her eyes as their pursuers sent out an endless spray of bullets, peppering several nearby buildings in the process. Lights flicked on in the houses, the bright windows spotlighting their position on the streets.

The taller man dropped back, returning fire and telling the curious to get back in their homes.

"We're almost there," L.T. assured her.

How could he still talk? Her mouth felt like she was breathing through sand, her feet heavy and aching. As he pulled her around another corner, her foot caught in the hem of her robe, and she flew to the ground, landing hard on her hands and knees.

L.T. didn't bother telling her to get up, instead lifting her to her feet. As soon as the soles of her shoes hit the ground, something screamed past her, setting her arm on fire. She grunted at the impact, stumbling three steps.

She waited for the feel of the ground against her side, preparing for the impact of another fall. But it never came. Instead, she was suddenly weightless, bouncing on L.T.'s shoulder, one of his arms wrapped around her legs.

"Try to hold still."

"All right." Easier said than done. It was quite possibly the most uncomfortable position in the world, each step jabbing her in the stomach. But at least she wasn't on her own feet anymore.

She let her arms hang down his back, trying to figure out what to do with her hands. Finally she grabbed his belt to give her something to hang on to, but her left arm was useless. She couldn't make her hand grasp anything.

What was dripping from her fingertips?

She rubbed her left thumb over her fingertips, which were slick and sticky.

It wasn't sweat.

She swallowed the bile that rose in her throat, refusing to wonder if it was from the awkward position or the blood dripping down her arm.

"ETA thirty seconds."

It took her a moment to realize he wasn't speaking to her, but relief washed through her as they rounded one last building, greeted by the gentle crashing of waves against the sandy shore. She couldn't see or hear them, but somehow she knew there were more soldiers waiting for them. More men like L.T.

L.T.'s steps slowed down as he splashed into the water. It was nearly to his knees by the time he stopped.

"We've got company," he said to one of the others as he swung her to his front, holding her back and under her knees and lifting her into what looked like a black inflated lifeboat. "She's been hit in the arm, but she hasn't lost consciousness."

He set her down on her back, but didn't let go of her hand. "You'll be fine now, Ms. Hayes." The boat floated toward open water, and he walked alongside it.

"Aren't you coming with us?" Her eyes suddenly filled with tears at the thought of not having her mysterious hero by her side. There hadn't been a chance before, but she'd thought that once they got away, she could tell him about what she'd seen, what she'd heard while she'd been held captive. Maybe he could help her.

"Not until you're safely out of range. Then we'll get out of here." He bobbed in time with the waves that must have been at least to his waist.

"Please." Her voice broke, but she pressed on. There wasn't much time. "Can you help me?" The crashing waves covered her words, but her grip never loosened, even as he relaxed his fingers.

"You're going to be okay." He pulled his hand away, his words assuaging none of her fears. "They'll take good care of you."

"Please." Her cry pierced the silent night. Her heart still raced, despite his words of comfort. She might be safe in the moment, but what about when she returned home? "He'll know that I know."

She tried to shout the words, but they barely came out as a whisper. The fear, the blood loss and the crashing adrenaline drained her last ounce of energy. Even though she was still in danger, she couldn't help but give in to exhaustion. Closing her eyes, everything went black.

TWO

Two weeks later

Staci ran her hand over the side of her face in a vain attempt to cover the still-red scar in front of her ear—left by a particularly unpleasant guard the day before her rescue. Forcing her hands back to her lap, she smoothed out the wrinkled lines of her skirt, tugging on the hem. After two years of following Lybanian laws and covering every inch of her body except her face, the skirt that hit below her knees felt too short.

She pulled the sleeves of her cardigan sweater down to her wrists in turn. Anything to keep her mind off the man she was waiting to see.

But he didn't know she was coming for a visit.

And she didn't even know his name.

The walls of the brightly lit office were devoid of windows, like the cell she'd endured for weeks. But this wasn't Lybania. It wasn't a cell.

She was free to leave.

Except she had to see him. The man who had rescued her. The only one who might agree to help her. She'd tried to talk to the public affairs officer assigned to the mission, a local policeman and even her congressman.

No one would take her seriously.

The public affairs officers hadn't even listened to her—too busy briefing her about the next interview.

The desk officer at her local precinct had agreed to take her statement but then had stared at her evidence with clear disinterest. To be sure, the foreign words on it probably looked like nothing more than scribbles to him, but she had hoped the map itself would make him take her seriously. It hadn't. The drawing had been too vague, too imprecise. Too easy to write off. He'd made a dismissive offer to pass the scrap of paper to a detective for review, but she wasn't about to leave the only evidence of the upcoming danger with a man who seemed more concerned with jaywalkers than terrorists.

As for her congressman… Well, his secretary had expressed appropriate concern for Staci's recent ordeal, but had made it clear that the congressman's calendar was full. The unspoken message was that the congressman had no time to deal with delusional constituents.

"It's normal for rescued hostages to deal with post-traumatic stress disorder," the PAO had said. "I can recommend a few very good counselors to help you deal with the stress of your ordeal and the ensuing media firestorm."

It wasn't stress. She wasn't hallucinating.

Her last chance was the lieutenant who had carried her to safety. Maybe he'd believe her. Maybe he could help her.

A woman at the commissary on base had told her that some of the SEALs of Team FIFTEEN had offices in this building.

She'd wait until she saw someone familiar. Or until someone realized she'd skipped out on the interview training she was supposed to be attending with the PAO and kick her out.

At the far end of a long hallway lined with offices, a

metal door clanged open, rattling the walls of the trailer. A swarm of men entered, laughing and pounding each other on the back, each in matching tan T-shirts and brown camouflage pants.

How could she possibly recognize her rescuer if they all looked alike?

What if he wasn't as handsome as she remembered? What if his eyes weren't as blue or his hair as boyishly tousled? Or his smile as kind and his features as perfectly put together as they had seemed to be under that black paint? After all, he'd ridden in like a knight on a white horse at a time when she was almost too afraid to think. He couldn't possibly be as attractive as her hazy memories of that night recalled.

The group of men drew near, clearly not aware of her presence, so she stood and grabbed on to the bottom of her sweater for support. Suddenly the short man at the front of the group stopped, holding up his hand to signal that all of the dozen or so should do the same. And they did, as if they'd practiced this single move every day for a year. Conversation ceased, and she quivered under the weight of so many eyes.

"How'd you get in here?"

She pointed over her shoulder, half turning toward the trailer's front door before thinking better of spilling the whole story. It was best to just ask for what she wanted to know. "I'm trying to find a lieutenant."

The man at the front squinted at her, his scowl growing. "We have a couple of those, but none you'd like very well. What are you doing here?"

"Oh, I'm looking for a specific one. But...well..." She stared at her clasped hands just long enough to build up the courage to look back into the wall of men. "I'm afraid I don't know his name. I'm Staci, Staci Hayes. And there was a SEAL, a lieutenant, I believe, who rescued me in Lybania."

"L.T., do you want to take this one?"

Like the Red Sea parting when Moses lifted his staff, the men moved against the walls until a familiar figure walked down the aisle. His gait easy and confident, he squinted at her until he'd reached the front of the pack, his hands resting loosely on his hips.

"Ms. Hayes, what can I do for you?"

She held out her hand, hoping he'd take it, hoping she looked less foolish than she felt.

He glanced down at her hand, and when his eyes rose, they stole her breath. There was no mistaking this was the man who had rescued her. His eyes weren't friendly, but they hadn't been two weeks ago, either. Then and now, they were focused and direct—taking in the situation at hand. At least she had his attention.

"I'm Staci." She pushed her hand farther forward, ignoring the lump in her throat as her fingers passed the halfway point between them.

He nodded to the group still congregated behind him. "They call me L.T." His eyes searched her face, finally lighting on her right side, on the scar that the doctor had said would probably always be visible.

She pulled back the hand that he obviously wasn't going to shake, and used it to cover the scar, staring at the floor in front of his feet. Apparently he wasn't going to give her his name, no matter how hard he stared at her. All right. She didn't need his name. Just his help.

"May we speak?" She glanced around his muscled shoulder—the same one she'd been slung over—into the faces of his men. "In private."

His face pinched for a moment, all the air in the trailer suddenly vanishing. Still he stared at her, his eyes roaming from her hair to her feet and back. It wasn't an obnoxious assessment, or even inappropriate. Clearly he was a man used to knowing what was coming, and her surprise visit didn't suit him.

The silence dragged on for what felt like hours, but all of the men remained motionless. She didn't even catch one blinking. Perfectly silent. Perfectly still.

By comparison, she felt like a camel in a crystal store, every straightening of her sweater or twitch of her neck amplified, every shuffle of her foot echoing to the farthest corner of the hall. But she couldn't seem to stop moving.

A strange habit she'd picked up during her time in captivity. Movement meant she was still alive. It gave her something to focus on in that pit, something to touch when she'd almost forgotten the feel of her own skin.

Now she was a hummingbird among ravens. Why couldn't she stop drawing attention to herself?

Wrapping her arms around her stomach, she held her breath and pinched her eyes closed until the man responded.

"All right." Her eyes flew open, and he nodded toward the nearest office with a wide window looking into the hallway.

He held out his hand, and she scurried in the direction he indicated. As she passed him, he cupped a hand under her elbow, and she flinched. Once he'd closed the door behind them, he spun on her, his eyes flashing with an intensity sharper than a sword. "Are you still injured?"

Her hand got to her shoulder before she realized she was going for her scar again. "No. Why do you ask?"

"Out there in the hallway, you flinched when I touched you. Did that hurt? Did the bullet do serious damage?"

"Oh." She bit her bottom lip. How was she supposed to explain that she still wasn't used to human touch? After three weeks of only painful interactions, even her mother's hug felt unnatural. "Um…no. It didn't hurt. The doctor on the aircraft carrier said it was a clean exit. I'm fine."

He ran his hand over his face, the sinewy muscles of his forearm bunching and pulling taut as he stared at the ceiling and blew out a slow breath. "Ms. Hayes, what are you doing here? This—" He flicked his finger back and forth between them. "This isn't allowed. You're not supposed to be here. We aren't supposed to communicate once the mission is over. Didn't the PAO tell you that?"

"I know."

"Where are you supposed to be right now?" His brows furrowed, compassion transforming his features.

She looked away from the Pacific blue of his eyes, her words caught in her throat.

"How'd you get on the base?"

She wheezed around the lump sitting on top of her airway, hugging her sweater in place. "I was supposed to have an interview prep course with the lieutenant commander in the public affairs office."

He marched to the far side of the desk, the only significant piece of furniture in the room, glanced at her over his shoulder and began pacing, hands grasped behind his back. "I understand that you've been through a serious ordeal, and I'm sorry that you had to go through that. But I'm not allowed any private contact with you." He scrubbed his face again with an open palm, still not looking in her direction.

It was easier to think and speak when he wasn't staring her down, so she rushed to tell him everything. "Do you remember the last thing I said to you that night?"

He stopped but kept his head straight forward. "I do." With the shake of his head, he ran his fingers through his pale brown hair. "You were under a lot of stress, and you'd been imprisoned for weeks. It isn't unusual to hallucinate under those kinds of conditions."

"I wasn't hallucinating."

He turned back toward her, but she couldn't meet his gaze. It was too disarming. So she looked around the room, searching for something—anything—to help steer this conversation where it needed to go.

Hugging her arms around her stomach, she took a deep breath. If she didn't lay it all on the line now, there might not be a later.

"You said I was safe. You said you'd protect me."

"I did. You made it safely home, didn't you?" His words were short but not unkind.

"I made it home, anyway."

Those blue eyes sliced into hers.

"What does that mean?" His lips barely moved.

"Someone has been following me, and I think it's the same man from Lybania."

"The one who will know that you know?" His arms crossed over his broad chest, the sleeves of his T-shirt pulling snug around his biceps. He looked so intimidating. If he hadn't leaned toward her, head cocked in concern, she'd have turned and run.

She nodded slowly. "Yes."

"Did you call the police? Tell them you're being stalked, and they can look into it for you. They can handle things like that."

"I did call the police. They wouldn't help me. I promise you're the last person I want to bother with this, but I don't have anywhere else to turn."

He sighed, dropping his hands to his side. "So, who is this guy?"

"Um…" She bit her lip and looked down at her sandals. "I don't know."

His eyebrows shot up his forehead, which wrinkled in even ripples. She could read the doubt on his face. He probably thought she saw a Middle Eastern man behind her in line for coffee, and that fear made her jump to the conclusion that he was following her. His voice dropped to almost a whisper. "I think you need to talk to someone about this. The PAO could probably recommend a counselor."

Her blood boiled at his condescension, and her apprehension evaporated. Taking a deep breath in through her nose, she pushed it out through tight lips.

If she had any idea how to face down the man following her on her own, she would. But since she didn't, she had to convince the lieutenant to help.

Taking a firm step toward him, she pointed her finger toward his chest, but stopped about two feet short of touching him. She wasn't that brave. "Listen to me. I'm in trouble, but it's not just me. I don't know the name of the man who's after me, but I know that I heard him plotting to blow up something here in San Diego."

"Do you speak Arabic?"

"Just enough to get by for two years in Lybania."

He squinted at her, leaning toward her still-outstretched finger. "Then how do you know you didn't misunderstand what he said?"

"He was speaking English."

Tristan snapped his full focus on Staci at her words. "Was he American?"

"Yes." She didn't hesitate.

Could she be telling the truth? "How do you know?"

"How would you know an American? He spoke like an American, used words like an American."

"Did he have an accent?"

She looked toward the ceiling, worrying her lip between

her teeth before answering. "Not that I noticed. He wasn't from the South or Boston or New Jersey. He sounded like a national newscaster, polished and smooth."

Rats. This girl honestly thought she'd overheard something. Whether she was really being stalked or not, there was no denying she thought she was in trouble.

But he wasn't the right one to help her. Getting involved in something like this could only spell trouble—mostly with his commanding officer, who had already warned him once about being too friendly with rescued hostages.

He scrubbed his fingers along his scalp, a vain attempt to relieve some of the pressure building there. She wasn't supposed to be there. He was breaking all the rules already by speaking one-on-one with a rescued hostage. If his CO found out, he'd be knee-deep in a serious mess, and no matter how pretty she was, she wasn't worth risking being grounded for the next mission or worse.

He didn't like telling a scared woman that he couldn't help her, but what other choice did he have? It was highly likely that the danger was all in her mind, even though she'd convinced herself that it was real. It would be wrong to give up the chance to go on missions that made a real difference just to help her fight imaginary enemies.

She flicked a strand of dark hair over her shoulder, blinking huge green eyes up at him. Her full, pink lips pressed together, wrinkling her nose slightly. It took everything inside him not to smile at her, to put her at ease and give her the assurance she craved.

But that wouldn't do either of them any good.

"Look, Ms. Hayes, I am sorry that you went through that experience. I'm sorry about what happened to you in Lybania, but I already did as much as I can for you. Now you have to keep living your life. Do you have a pastor or priest you could talk with? Maybe he could help you work through this."

Her shoulders fell, the last remnant of hope in her features vanishing. "All right. Thank you for your time."

She turned, shuffling toward the office door, and a band around his heart squeezed. He'd done the right thing sending her away. So why did it feel so wrong?

Just as she reached the door, she tucked a hand into the pocket of her colorful skirt. As she spun on the spot, she held out something that she'd pulled from within. "I almost forgot. One of the guards dropped this in my cell after talking to the American man."

He reached for the scrap of paper and unfolded it to reveal a crude sketch.

"Doesn't it look kind of like—"

"—the harbor," he finished for her. There could be no doubt about the docks and shoreline. He'd run along the beaches in the sketch for nearly ten years. He knew every ship and slip.

And apparently someone else did, too.

"But I don't know what that says." She pointed toward a line of scrawled symbols.

He squinted at the text. "It's not Arabic, but it's not far off, either." He pointed to the third and fourth word on the page. "This looks like one and two, but it's not. It's different."

"You read Arabic?"

He glanced up from the words written on the map. "Enough." That was a bit of an understatement. He was actually almost fluent in it and could read nearly anything. But she didn't need to know that. A few secrets always came in handy.

"I think it's a dialect from the hill country. I only picked up a few words of the different dialects while I was there, but it would seem to fit."

He nodded. "Might be right." So why was someone writing in Lybanese on a map of his harbor? His gut clenched as he realized her story might be true after all. But why would they be after Staci? Who would think her a real threat?

"What did you overhear exactly?"

Her eyes shone for just a moment before she blinked her hope back under control. "One of the guards said something about the pieces needed to build the bomb. He said they had almost everything they needed, and when it went off, everyone would know they wouldn't be intimidated by America's military. And then the American said he'd place it, and it would be just like fireworks."

That wasn't much to go on. "What else?"

She chewed her lip again, running a finger over the side of her face for the tenth time. "I guess they were talking about this map. I think the American was pointing out landmarks and such."

"Then what happened?"

"They were still talking when someone else came into my cell."

His stomach jolted, his hands forming fists completely on their own. He didn't want to know, but he had to ask. "What did he do?"

"He tried to get me to confess to breaking the law by giving away bibles. When I wouldn't confess, he left and the other guy, the one who had been talking to the American, came in to take his turn. He was angry I wouldn't give in, and I don't think he noticed when he dropped the map. I scooped it up when he had his back turned. After that, everything is kind of fuzzy until you showed up."

"You mean, this all happened the day of your rescue?"

She nodded.

"Did the Timmonses hear the American, too?"

"No." She locked her hands in front of her, her skirt swishing like a bell as she swayed. "They had separated us after our second week."

"Why?"

She looked away, and he felt the gut punch as sure as if one of the other guys on his team had thrown it. That was a stupid question. Pretty girls in Lybania being held by ruthless terrorists…

He'd seen enough of that country to know, and he could only pray that she'd been spared the worst, that her physical scars were deeper than her emotional and spiritual ones.

His pulse pounded in his ears, suddenly ready for a fight. But he'd already taken on the guys responsible for the pink spreading over her cheeks and the bright red scar in front of her ear that she kept trying to cover.

"It wasn't anything like what…" Her voice trailed off, and she cleared her throat. "That is, they were waiting for someone. For their leader, I think." The pink in her cheeks turned into flames.

Thank God his team had rescued her when it had.

But even if she'd avoided the physical attack, knowing what was coming had to have left a few emotional scars. It was brave of her to have taken the map in the first place. At a time when she'd been at such high risk herself, she'd thought of others, and had tried to gather evidence she'd hoped to use to keep people safe. That said a lot about her. And it made him even more reluctant to turn her away.

Maybe he could look into this in his free time. He didn't have any training missions on the schedule for the next few weeks. Could it hurt to at least keep his eyes and ears open for an American placing a bomb somewhere in San Diego that would send a message to America's military?

It was a huge city and highly unlikely he'd see anything, but at least he could put her mind at ease.

"I'll see what I can do."

"You will?" Her voice skyrocketed, and she plastered a smile into place.

"Yes." He looked at the door then back at her. "Leave me your phone number, and I'll call you if I find out anything."

"And how should I contact you?"

"Through your PAO. She'll pass any messages to me."

"And who should I ask her to pass them to?"

She hadn't missed a beat and was intent on getting his name. "Lieutenant Sawyer."

"All right." She scribbled her phone number on a sticky note and handed it to him before opening the office door. "Thank you, Lieutenant Sawyer. For two weeks ago and for today."

"You're welcome, Ms. Hayes."

"Please call me Staci."

"All right."

As she flounced out the door, he couldn't tear his eyes away from her. Her dark curls bounced with every step, her shoulders in perfect posture. She may have sustained a flesh wound to the arm and a cut on her face, but her three weeks as a hostage hadn't damaged her backbone.

When the outside door of the trailer clanged shut, he walked back to his office, ignoring the stares of Willie G. and Zach—Zig—McCloud.

Zig whistled low and long, elbowing his teammate in the ribs. "I guess it pays to have rank. I'd go to the academy, too, if I had pretty girls like that coming to thank me."

"What'd she give you?"

Tristan clutched the scrap of paper in his hand, forcing down the knot in his stomach. It shouldn't matter that they were teasing him. He'd sure teased them over the past couple years.

But Staci Hayes wasn't a SEAL groupie. She didn't hang around the pool hall waiting for a SEAL to show up. She hadn't gone looking for a warrior.

He'd gone looking for her.

And she deserved better than the speculation of two of his men. "Willie G. and Zig, go clean up the training boats."

Zig opened his mouth, about ready to argue, then realized that it wasn't a request but an order.

"Yes, sir."

They stalked off, leaving him some time alone with the crude map and a head full of questions. As he sank into his desk chair and leaned back until it popped, he replayed Staci's words over and over. Had there really been an American man consorting with Lybanian terrorists? If so, where on this map were they planning to place the bomb they'd mentioned? And what did the message on the map really mean? Thousands of hours practicing languages were useless if he couldn't read the one in front of him.

The map didn't contain a convenient X to mark the spot or even a circle to pinpoint which part of the coast might see the explosion. But it did contain the coastline of Coronado Island. From the airport to the naval stations, Harbor Drive, and even the golf course.

It represented too many people. Too many possible victims.

And he had nowhere to start.

The best he could do was a call to a friend in the FBI's counterterrorism unit and a former cryptology instructor for the navy.

After leaving messages with just enough information to get him a return call, he shut down his computer and grabbed his bag of workout gear, slinging it over his shoulder as he strolled out of the building and past the two SEALs hosing down a rack of RIBs—Rigid Inflatable Boats.

"Have a good weekend, boys." He waved, not even trying to hide his smirk as he reached the parking lot. Throwing his bag into the bed of his truck, he jumped up, sliding behind the wheel.

As he pulled onto the main street that ran most of the length of the naval station, he tried to focus on the rare two-day weekend ahead of him.

He'd promised his sister, Ashley, that he'd put together the crib for his soon-to-arrive nephew. And she wanted to do some more shopping for baby clothes before Matt—her husband as well as Tristan's senior chief—returned from demo training in Chicago.

Maybe she'd let him off the hook for the shopping trip if he put together the crib and matching dresser.

He waved a civilian pedestrian across the walkway. She was halfway to the next parking lot over before he realized she was his afternoon visitor. She was coming from the administrative offices, probably just finished with the interview training to prep her for upcoming media appearances about her ordeal. He'd already seen her picture in the papers, but she'd yet to make a morning show appearance. Lt. Commander del Rey, the PAO, was probably talking Staci through the schedule.

Staci slid into her green sedan and pulled out of her spot, winding between the thinning crowd of other vehicles. She had reached the exit of the parking lot by the time the white delivery van behind Tristan honked.

He laughed at himself for being so easily distracted and waved out the window, pulling up to one of the guardhouses at the front gate of the base.

"Carl, how you doing, man?"

The broad-shouldered Samoan snapped to attention in the door frame of the little hut. "Good. How about you, Lieutenant Sawyer? How's your sister?"

"Oh, you know. Waterstone took off to Chicago for training, so Ashley moved back in with me in case the kid comes early."

Carl laughed. "You know any kid of the senior chief's is going to show up early."

Tristan's shoulders shook as he waved at the younger man and pulled off the base, right behind a green four-door with a rusted bumper.

He tried to catch a glimpse of her chestnut hair, just to make sure it was Staci, but from the seat in his truck, he couldn't confirm. It didn't stop him from following her over the bridge and into San Diego traffic.

He passed an exit for I-5, which he should have taken to pick up Ashley.

So why was he following someone he wasn't supposed to have any individual contact with? He didn't have a good reason, just an instinct telling him to make sure she got home safely.

A glance in his rearview mirror showed the same white van from the base still on his six. It hung back but took every turn he did. Every turn the green car did.

His gut clenched after the third turn.

There was only one way to know for sure who the van was following.

At the next cross street Tristan slowed down and put on his blinker to turn right. The green car pulled almost a block ahead as he turned onto the side street. As soon as he'd cleared the turn, the white van gunned it past Tristan's truck.

Somehow he'd ended up literally in the middle of something, and now that he was out of the way, that van had a clear shot at the green car. At Staci.

He shoved his gear shift into Reverse and slammed on the gas, spinning the steering wheel and completing a full one-eighty before turning right back onto the main road. In one quick motion he took off after them, joined only by the smell of burning rubber.

He caught up to the van about four blocks later as it maneuvered itself to pin the sedan against the deserted sidewalk in front of the gated entrance of a convenience store.

Air caught in his throat until he schooled it into measured breaths, keeping his hands steady despite the rush of adrenaline that coursed from the top of his head to his fingertips.

Like it or not, he was part of this now. No way was he going to let a fool in a van hurt the girl he'd risked his neck to rescue on the other side of the world.

The van let up for a moment, and Tristan hoped he might be able to get between the two vehicles. But his hopes were in vain. A second later, the van crashed into the side of the green car, sending it careening into a light pole.

THREE

Staci jerked against the shoulder strap of her seat belt, which stole her breath but kept her head from cracking against the steering wheel. The car was too old to have air bags. There was nothing but the seat belt to protect her.

With one eye pinched closed and the other only open partway, she surveyed the white van with tinted windows as it sped away after running her into the light pole. As she clawed at the seat-belt buckle and fought for air, she sank against the steering wheel, every ounce of strength dripping from the bottom of her feet through the floorboard.

Maybe if she held her head between her hands, the world would stop spinning.

And maybe if the world would stop spinning, she could pull her thoughts together.

She pressed her palms harder into her forehead, but the earth still seemed to be whirling out of control. As she fell toward her car door, it suddenly disappeared, replaced by a pair of hands that cradled her against a broad chest.

"Whoa there."

The voice was deep and strong like the hands, but she couldn't manage to open her eyes far enough to look into his face.

"Did you hit your head?"

She rubbed it absently, unable to pinpoint if the pain came from the spinning inside or a throbbing outside. "I don't think so." The last word came out on a wheeze, and she pushed against the cotton covering his shoulder—his unmovable shoulder—for any ounce of space.

"Careful." He loosened his grip, but not enough.

She managed a shallow breath. "I'm okay."

"I'm not so sure about that. Just stay with me for a second."

Something about his words pricked at her memory. They were familiar like a sweet dream.

"Stay with you." She swallowed and gasped for air and with it the strength to open her eyes.

The arch of his nose and curve of his mouth were just as surprising—and welcome—as the first time she'd seen them.

"Lieutenant Sawyer?"

He shrugged the shoulder where her hand still rested. "Hello." His eyes twinkled, and something akin to humor crossed his face. "We've got to stop meeting this way."

"Why are you here?" But it didn't really matter.

"Well…" His lips puckered to the side, a row of fine lines wrinkling his forehead as he stewed on her question. "Just in the right place at the right time."

"Guess this means it's all real, isn't it?"

For a moment he looked as if he were going to play dumb, pretend he didn't understand what she meant, but as she blinked up at his face, he nodded. "I guess so. But I wouldn't worry about it. We'll find him."

Any other day, any other situation, she'd have argued with him. He was trying to pacify her, but she didn't need it. At the moment, though, she just needed to lean into him and let him make sure she got home in one piece.

So she did.

* * *

"Thank you for your help. I don't know how I'd have gotten home without you."

Tristan stood two inches inside the front door of Staci's town house on the hardwood of the entryway, staring into a sea of white. Her carpet, furniture and curtains. All of it gleamed.

Hadn't she ever had a dog? Or a kid brother? Or a visitor?

Sterile as a hospital room.

"Sure thing. No problem."

She looked toward the back of the house, crossing her arms over her chest and grabbing her opposite shoulders. "Can I get you a glass of water or a soda?"

"No, thanks. I should get going." He motioned to the door. "The paramedic said you should try to get some rest. You'll probably be pretty sore tomorrow."

Just as his hand connected with the doorknob, she grabbed his other arm—then dropped it as if he burned her fingers. "What do I do if he comes after me again?"

He let go of the door and reached to give her elbow a reassuring squeeze before letting his hand fall to his side. She sure hadn't appreciated his touch that afternoon. "I doubt he knows where you live. Is your name on this property?"

"No. My parents bought it as an investment property a couple years before I left for Lybania. A friend of mine stayed here while I was gone."

That was good. Anyone could look up property owners in the county recorder's office, but Hayes was a common name. "You'll be safe. And your car will be in the shop for at least a week, so he won't be able to use it to ID where you live. Do you have someone who can run errands for you, if you need?"

"Yes."

"Then you're all set."

"But what if..."

Her tone gouged at his stomach, and he couldn't walk away. She wasn't playing the part of a lost little girl nor tempting him with her feminine charm. Fear shook her voice, and those three little words carried a heavy weight of meaning.

She knew the truth as clearly as he did.

Someone was after her. And until he was caught, she wouldn't be safe.

He closed his eyes, fighting the urge to do what he'd done in Lybania. But he couldn't just pick her up and carry her to safety. He wasn't supposed to have any contact with her. And explaining to his CO that he'd watched her get run off the road wasn't going to change the rule.

She would be safe enough in her home for now. And he could turn this whole thing over to his buddy in the FBI.

But he couldn't walk away from the tremor in her voice.

"If something happens, call me." He moved his hand as though he was wielding a pen. "Do you have something to write on?"

She shuffled papers in a mail organizer, finally pulling out a white envelope with a clear, plastic window, shoving the paper and a pencil into his hands. He scribbled his number down and handed it back to her.

She smiled, the light never quite reaching her eyes. "Thank you."

"You're welcome." He turned to go but stopped with the door only partially open. "Try to get some rest this weekend."

She followed him to the cement slab that could hardly be called a porch, despite its overhang. "All right."

He made it to the last of three steps before her voice stopped him again.

"Wait."

He glanced over his shoulder, squinting into her soft features, her pink lips glistening in the evening sun.

"If I have to phone, what do I call you?" She held the envelope in front of her.

"L.T. is fine."

"How can I trust you if I don't even know your first name?"

His eyes narrowed and his nostrils flared. The last time a woman had tried so hard to get his first name, the first use she'd made of it had been to ask him out on the date that started a one-year-long relationship. She'd said his name so sweetly before she'd kissed him, slow and thorough.

That last time.

Before he'd boarded a transport and left her all by herself.

But Staci wasn't Robin. And she certainly wouldn't be kissing him. If there wasn't a first, then there couldn't be a last kiss.

"Tristan. But hardly anyone calls me that."

"Why not?"

He put his hands on his hips, still squinting up at her from the bottom of the steps. "They just don't. Everyone on the team has a nickname, and we use them."

"All right." She took a breath then quickly added, "L.T.," as if it were an afterthought. And for a split second he wished she'd called him by his real name. "Thank you."

She waved the envelope again, and he jogged toward his truck, suddenly eager to be away from the woman who made him think about memories that were best forgotten.

Staci left her cereal bowl on the kitchen counter at the sound of the doorbell, pulling the belt of her robe tighter around her waist as she shuffled toward the front door. Peering through the windows on both sides of the entry, she confirmed that her tiny porch was empty before unlocking the deadbolt and opening the door just enough to look into the morning sun.

The delivery man must have run back to his truck, leaving only a package by the front mat. As she bent to pick it up, every muscle in her body screamed. She groaned against the pain in her ribs and chest as her muscles flexed and tightened.

Wasn't she supposed to be feeling better? Three days was plenty of time to recover from a car accident that didn't even break her skin. Right?

She hefted the box, nearly dropping the unexpected weight and falling right alongside it.

Maybe three days wasn't quite long enough.

Another try boasted better results, and she held the package against her stomach to ease the pressure on her strained back as she pushed the door closed behind her. Setting the brown paper-wrapped package on her counter, she spied the return label.

From Rebecca Meyers.

Why was her sister, Becca, sending her a package when they'd seen each other a week ago? And why had she spelled out her whole name? They'd been calling each other by their first initials since she was ten. Even now, B's kids called her Auntie S. And even if she were going to use her name instead of her initial, Becca had never actually gone by Rebecca.

Her stomach lurched and she pressed a hand to it, suddenly uninterested in the cereal still floating in its milk.

Staci pushed the package toward the far end of the counter, staring hard at the brown paper bag used to wrap the box. Hadn't B given up paper and plastic in favor of more environmentally friendly reusable bags?

So many things about this weren't right.

She grabbed her phone and punched in her sister's phone number. After four rings, B's melodic voice sing-songed, "This is Becca Meyers. Sorry I missed you. You know what to do, and I'll get back to you as soon as I can."

"Hey, B. It's just me. Just…um…" No cause to scare her sister. Nope. She could handle this. "Just wanted to tell you that I love you. Talk to you later."

As she pressed the end button on her phone, her gaze flicked toward the white envelope stuck to the refrigerator, and her heart skipped a beat at the very thought of calling Tristan—L.T.

What if the box on her counter was nothing? Then she'd look stupid for taking up his time with something ridiculous. But then, what if it was something dangerous?

She backed up until she bumped into the kitchen island and then swung around that. Putting the waist-high counter between her and the package wasn't enough, so she kept going, hoping she might suddenly get X-ray vision if she tried hard enough.

No such luck.

After a five-minute showdown with the box, she doubled her fists beneath her chin, took a deep breath and stepped back toward the counter. She'd never know what was inside if she didn't open it.

The paper was thick and coarse as she picked it back up. And set it right back down, her heart thumping and ears ringing.

"You're being silly." She meant to encourage herself, but it backfired.

She'd been held hostage, had overheard a plot to blow up something and been run off the road. If being silly meant being cautious about the chance of danger, then this was the time for silliness.

Snatching the envelope from the fridge, she punched the numbers into her phone. On the second ring: "L.T."

"This is Staci." She quickly added, "Hayes. Staci Hayes."

She could almost hear the sigh in his voice and see the sag in his shoulders. "What can I do for you?"

"Someone dropped a box off on my front porch this morning, and it has my sister's return address. But I don't think she sent it."

"Why not?"

"She used her whole name."

"Her whole name?" His tone clearly asked "Are you serious?" even if his words didn't.

Of course she was serious. "We've always gone by nicknames, but the return address has her whole name on it. And it's wrapped in a brown paper bag, which she'd never use."

"How big is the box?" His voice picked up like she had his attention.

She held her hand along the side of the box. "About eight inches by eight inches."

He must have pressed his hand over his phone, but she could still hear his words as he leaned away from it. "Willie G., get Zig and River and the bomb kit. Meet me at my truck in two minutes."

Her stomach dropped and she scrambled back, tripping over her own feet to get out of the kitchen and away from the unknown threat. Her phone fell from limp fingers and bounced on the hardwood floor.

It squawked at her as her gaze shifted back and forth between the brown box and her black phone. She didn't have to pick it up. She could just run. Get out of the house and call the police.

Or she could stick around and figure out who was behind her car accident and the most recent unwelcome gift.

Scooping up her phone was as painful as picking up the bomb had been. Whether from the bruise across her sternum or the rush of blood to her head, every one of her muscles throbbed.

"Staci? Are you still there?" L.T. sounded impatient.

"I dropped my phone."

"Listen." His tone turned softer than she'd ever heard it, yet he was still completely in control. "I need you to stay calm. Put as much distance as possible between you and that box. But do not go outside."

She glanced down at her ratty robe. "Why?"

"Do you remember when I got you out of Lybania, and I told you to do everything I said without question?"

She nodded, her gaze still locked on the special delivery.

"Stay with me. You've got to do the same thing now. Trust me. We'll be there in twenty minutes. Just go into your bathroom, close the door and get into the bathtub."

"All right." Her throat refused to swallow, dry and tight. "Twenty minutes?"

"Nineteen." Something—probably his truck—roared to life. "Do you want me to stay on the phone with you?"

"I'm okay. I'll leave the door unlocked."

He hung up without pomp, but her feet refused to move.

What if the box exploded while she stood there, tearing her home and body to shreds?

The police would find her shrouded in bits of ratty bath robe.

That was enough to get her moving, running to her room and slipping into workout pants and a long-sleeved shirt. And then into the tub.

The porcelain was hard against her back as she pulled her knees up to her chin and waited for her world to explode. She'd never get to be the aunt she wanted to be to her nieces. She'd never even have a chance to get married. She'd never know if there was a man willing to marry her despite what she couldn't give him.

All because of that man. That man who was planning to bomb her in San Diego was also stealing her future.

She smacked her mouth against the bitterness rising in her heart and squeezed her hands into fists.

The sea-foam-green wall above the sink did nothing to calm her boiling ire, so she pinched her eyes closed and pressed her fists over her ears.

"God, don't let me be this angry so close to meeting You."

The words hurt her throat, but she whispered them again and again, praying for a release from the fear intent on inciting her deepest-seated resentment.

"Staci, it's L.T." Though his voice came from the direction of the front door, it carried to every corner of her house.

"I'm in here. In the bathroom. Like you said."

A herd of bison ran through the foyer toward the kitchen, but she didn't hear anyone approach her haven until the doorknob turned and popped open. Like he had the first time she saw him, Tristan filled the doorway. But this time, he leaned against the jamb and crossed his arms, his blue eyes narrow.

As he stood there, not saying a word, she shifted over and over again, the weight of his gaze making the bathtub even more uncomfortable.

She grasped for something to say. Anything.

But words failed in the face of the man who looked

completely at ease while she huddled as far away from the package as she could.

Finally he broke the silence, his voice as casual as if they were making small talk in a church foyer. "What time did it arrive?"

"Um…" There was too much going on. How could she be responsible for remembering the details, too? She pinched her eyes closed and tried to remember. "Maybe ten minutes before I called you."

"All right."

After the short exchange, the silence physically hurt, pressing on her shoulders as she waited. Even if she had no idea what she was waiting for. "Before, on the phone, you told me not to go outside. Why?"

He glanced behind him before responding. "Any assassin worth his salt would wait around to make sure his delivery did its job. You'd have been a sitting target outside."

"Oh." The word had no volume, just wide eyes and an open mouth. "Did you see him when you got here?"

L.T. shook his head. "We did a quick sweep, but didn't see anything unusual." He shrugged a shoulder, his brown T-shirt stretching tight around the muscles in his arms. "Who knows? Maybe it's nothing."

Maybe he was right. Maybe she was overreacting.

Except he'd rushed over with a team of SEALs.

He didn't really think it was nothing.

"L.T.," one of the men called from the kitchen.

L.T. turned his back to her, but didn't move toward the kitchen. "What is it?"

"A pipe."

The taut muscles of his back flexed, but his voice didn't change pitch. "Take care of it."

"Will do."

When he turned back toward her, L.T. still wore a

Sunday-morning-church expression, calm and easygoing. "Do you want to scoot over?"

Her heart hammered, shaking every part of her. "Why? What's a pipe?"

"Just move over." He waved her to the side.

She slid toward the drain and faucet and he stepped into the tub, sinking down and somehow folding his long legs into the cramped space. His face twisted when he was finally in place, his shoulder just three inches from hers.

"Are you scared?" She wrapped her arms around her stomach.

"No." So nonchalant. So confident. "But I figured you might be getting lonely in here. And if that thing explodes, I want to be right by your side."

FOUR

Staci gulped a breath as Tristan put his arm around her shoulders. It was too intimate, too familiar, but she didn't have a choice but to go along with it. Getting out of the tub meant exposing herself to the force of a potential explosion.

"Are they going to be okay?"

He frowned at her, the blue of his eyes turning stormy like the Pacific in a hurricane. "They're pros. You'll be fine."

She shook her head, her hair flopping over her shoulder. "I'm not worried about me. I'm asking about them. Will those guys in my kitchen be okay if the bomb goes off?"

He squinted at her, lines forming between his eyebrows. Pinching the end of his nose until his fingers slipped free, he nodded two quick bobs. "They'll be fine. They're trained."

"Then why are we in here?"

"Contingency plan."

She pulled away from the weight of his arm across her shoulders, a chill running down her back at the loss of heat in the absence of his embrace. "Which means that something could go wrong and someone could be hurt. I can't let someone be hurt because of me."

Rubbing fingers on either side of the bridge of his nose,

he let out a slow breath, his shoulders falling on the exhale. "Don't sweat it. This is what we do. The chances of anything going wrong are almost nil. Ziggy is almost as good with explosives as Rock."

"Ziggy and the Rock?"

"Just Rock. You met him in Lybania. He's my senior chief."

Images from that night flooded her mind, every scene playing with precision across the back of her eyelids. L.T. had burst into her cell. And then there had been another man. "The one with the gun out in front of us?"

"That's right. He's doing some training on the other side of the country right now. But Zig is the next best man for the job. He's been blowing stuff up since he was thirteen."

"What?" Her voice squeaked as it shot up an octave, right along with her eyebrows that reached for her hairline.

He laughed, the sound full and throaty. "I don't mean he'll blow up your kitchen." He added a wink as he patted the top of her knee. "He just knows how things blow better than most. Which means he knows how to keep things from blowing better than them, too."

"And his name is Zig?" Maybe it was a family name, but who would saddle their child with a name guaranteed to get him teased?

"No. It's Zach McCloud."

He'd told her a few days before that the SEALs called each other by nicknames. "So how did he get the name Zig?"

"You'll understand when you meet him."

"How—"

A bald head poked in around the door frame. "All clear." The rest of his body—broad shoulders, arms laced with muscles and long legs—followed into the doorway.

Tristan pressed his palms against the edge of the tub

and popped to his feet before wrapping his long, callused fingers around her wrist and pulling with a quick burst that had her standing—and far too close to his chest—before she could do it herself.

"You're safe now, ma'am." The bald head shone in the bright bathroom lights as the other man offered part bow, part nod.

"Zig?"

"Yes, ma'am."

She lifted one leg to step out of the tub, L.T. cupping her elbow with a grip just firm enough to catch her should she slip. Giving him a tentative smile, she turned back to Zig. "I'm hardly old enough to be called ma'am. Don't you think?"

His big brown eyes twinkled, although the expression on his face never shifted from stoic calm. "Yes, ma'am."

"Well, then, Zig. Tell me how you got your nickname."

Again his eyes glimmered with otherwise unseen humor. He rubbed a flat hand over the dome of his head. "Guess I reminded the instructors of their favorite cartoon."

She frowned, pressing her hands to her hips. The tall, lean man looked as much like the short, plump cartoon as a peacock looked like a guinea pig. There was no comparison. He was the type of man who would have made Judy elbow her in the side and whisper something about finding a good husband.

L.T. stepped out of the tub behind her, his breath brushing the top of her head and sweeping a whole different kind of chill down her spine. She didn't need Judy there to tell her *he* was a good man.

She also didn't need another reminder why she had no business thinking along those lines.

When Chris had broken up with her, he had made it explicitly clear why she'd never be good enough for him or any other man. It shouldn't matter to her that good men were hard to find. She wasn't in the market for one anyway.

Zig's eyes swung toward L.T., the humor there vanishing. "You want to see it?"

"Yes." L.T. moved around her, and she fell into step behind him. Before they reached the bathroom door, he stopped and spun around. "Where are you going?"

"To the kitchen. With you."

"Uh-uh." He shook his head so hard his neck popped. "You don't need to see or hear this."

"Yes, I do."

He huffed out a breath between tight lips. "Listen to me, Staci. This isn't something that you want in your mind." He cupped a hand around her shoulder, holding her still to make her meet his eyes, to see how serious he was. "This is the stuff nightmares are made of, and you don't want to see any of it. It'll make you scared to live in your own home."

She pressed the tips of her fingers into her palms and tried for a lighter tone. "That's funny. I'm already scared in my own home."

As the words sprang out of her mouth, she knew their truth. The only secure place she had in the entire world wasn't safe anymore. Seeing the remnants of a bomb that was meant to injure her wasn't going to change that.

"I'm the pro here." His fingers squeezed gently. "Remember what I told you in Lybania. I need you to trust me on this."

She stared hard into his eyes, fighting the urge to blink away from the intensity there and break their standoff. "I'm already in danger. At least if I know what to look for, maybe I can keep my eyes open and recognize another threat."

His lips pursed to the side, his forehead a sea of wrinkles.

"Please. I need to know what I'm facing."

"All right." He turned and walked toward the kitchen, and she shadowed him the whole way there.

There were three others standing around the island, filling every nook and using up all of the oxygen in the room. Her head swam, her legs abruptly unstable, and she tripped as she reached the counter.

Again, L.T. came to her rescue, righting her with a rock-solid hand around her arm without even looking at her. He and Zig joined the conversation around a colorful pile of wires laying on the brown-paper wrapping.

"Go ahead." L.T. nodded to his men, and the weight of three pairs of eyes shifted from her shoulders. "What did you find?"

The youngest guy bobbed his mop of messy hair. "Whoever made this is a pro."

She shot a quick glance at L.T. out of the corner of her eye. His attention never wavered from the kid, who didn't look old enough to be out of college, let alone a SEAL.

Zig leaned forward and pointed to one of the wires. "He had a fail-safe in case this one didn't do the job. I nearly missed it. It was wrapped up and under here." He pressed a finger to the lip of a pipe. "But it wasn't just a detonator. It was an incinerator."

"You ever see anything like that?"

Zig nodded, his motion deliberate and thoughtful. "I had an instructor once talk about using this extra wire as both a fail-safe and to ignite an incinerator, but I've never seen it used before in practice. Like I said. He's a pro. And downright creative."

Staci swallowed at the lump in her throat, taking a tiny step toward the warmth radiating from L.T. "Why would there be an incinerator?"

L.T. met her gaze, his facial features motionless and

benign. But she couldn't tear her eyes away from his. She felt him take hold of her hand and latch on tight.

Zig cleared his throat behind a fist. "In this case, the incinerator makes the whole thing look like an accident."

She blinked twice at L.T., pain rocketing across her forehead from one temple to the other. Apparently he could read her mind, because his lips barely moved as he explained, "It would have blown so hard and fast that the wrapping, pipe and igniter wouldn't have been distinguishable from anything else in your house. It would have looked like a gas explosion, and no one would have known to look for a bomber."

Her hands curled into fists, but he didn't flinch as she squeezed his fingers.

The youngest team member shrugged. "Guess that explains why there wasn't a sniper outside, huh?"

L.T. shot the kid a glare that would have wilted flowers. "Not now, Willie."

As the lieutenant swung his gaze back to her, Staci squeezed his hand and borrowed as much strength as she could from him.

"What does that mean?"

"I'm not exactly sure."

She squinted at him, and he lifted one shoulder. "Not really, anyway. All I know for sure at this moment is that someone wants you out of the way. And he wants it to look like an accident."

Tristan immediately regretted telling Staci the entire truth. Her face turned white, and her hand shook in spite of its tight grip on his.

She didn't need to know the lengths that someone would go to to get rid of her. It would have been enough that Tristan and his team were aware of the real threat. Someone definitely wanted Staci out of the way, most likely because he thought that she had enough intel to stop him from reaching his ultimate objective.

Tristan patted her shoulder with his free hand, hoping against hope that she wouldn't dissolve into tears. Sure, he had practice thanks to his sister, Ashley, who was prone to emotional outbursts. Even if she claimed they were a result of her pregnancy. But he could barely handle a weepy Ashley, and he didn't have a clue what to do with a near stranger in a crying fit.

Staci took a shaking breath, straightening her shoulders and letting go of him to lock her hands in front of her. After several quick flutters of her long lashes, she cleared her throat. "Well, that's going to put a damper on my reacclimation."

Zig and Willie let loose with laughs so loud that they almost dwarfed her hesitant grin. But her smile wouldn't be thwarted so easily, and she glanced up at him out of the corner of her eye. The lift in the corner of her mouth showed off just a few white teeth and tugged on the puckered skin along the red scar in front of her ear.

He offered her a matching half smile. "I guess it would."

What was this woman like in the real world? In the grit of an op, in the face of a death threat, she followed orders and then cracked jokes.

But what about on a sunny Sunday afternoon? Did she like to walk barefoot on the beach? Or sit in a comfy chair, reading a book? Or snuggle on the couch in front of a football game?

Her gaze flicked from his face to the dismantled bomb and back, her posture tightening just enough for him to notice. The device was useless now, but the pile of wires still had enough power to make her uncomfortable in her own home.

"Zig, why don't you and the guys take that out to the truck?" He motioned toward the brown wrapper. "I'll be right behind you."

Willie wiggled his eyebrows but stayed blessedly silent as the three men scooped up the dismembered pieces and marched toward the front door, closing it so silently behind them that Staci looked around his shoulder to make sure it had been pulled tight.

When she was certain they were alone, she crossed her arms over her chest, sinking against the counter, using it to hold her up. He'd done that for her a time or two. He'd kept her standing and running in Lybania and kept her from hitting the ground after her car accident.

And if the sudden pinch in his gut was an indicator, he wouldn't mind having that job again.

And that was a dangerous attitude to have.

His CO had always been clear about the rules surrounding rescue missions. Tristan's anonymity was paramount. He'd seen the commander lay into SEALs who'd played loose and fast with pictures on social media, posting hints to their role on the teams and leaving the kids too visible to go undercover.

The rescued was the story. Not the rescuer.

And outside of all of that, there was still the personal reason. He knew how exciting and romantic women *thought* it would be to date a SEAL. And he also knew just how risky those relationships could be. It wasn't just a question of the danger he had to face, or the secrets he had to keep, even from the ones he loved the most. No, the hardest part was just how often he was away. How many birthdays he missed, how many anniversaries went uncelebrated. How many times someone he loved needed him at home, when instead he was half a world away. If he couldn't trust himself to be there to take care of the woman he loved, then he had no right to get involved in the first place. He'd learned that the hard way, and he sure didn't need any reminders.

If he were a smart man—and graduating at the top of his class at the Naval Academy suggested he was—he'd walk away from Staci Hayes before his head got filled with dumb ideas like trying to be the guy who'd be there for her on a permanent basis.

He could help her get set up in a safe place and call his linguistics instructor again to see if he could translate the words on the map. He'd keep an eye out and alert the right authorities to make sure someone followed up on the tip.

Hopefully it would all be resolved soon, and then he'd be free to forget this mission altogether. He'd already done more than anyone could expect.

"So, what do we do now?" She licked her lips, twirling the end of a long curl around her finger, and tugging until it bounced back into place.

We?

A rope around his lungs tightened, pinching his chest. When had they become a "we"?

He stepped back. Putting a few more feet between them couldn't hurt. After ten minutes in the tub, enough time to memorize the sweet scent of her perfume, he needed to get far enough away to think about anything other than tropical fruits.

"You should go someplace safe until this guy is caught. Do you have a relative you can stay with?"

Her lips pursed to the side, her brows lowering over her jade-green eyes. "But he knows who they are. At least who my sister is. I'm not going to stay with her or anyone else and put them in jeopardy. If he came after me, my family would be in danger, right?"

She had a point. The guy had done his homework.

"What about a friend or college roommate or someone you wouldn't be easily connected with?"

She shook her head. "Most of them have families now, too. And even if it was safe for them, which I would never risk, what about finding the man responsible for all this? Don't you think I should be close by so that I can help identify him? After all, I'm the only one who's heard his voice."

"But you've never seen him, right?"

"Well, not his face."

He cocked his head to the side. This was new. "What part of him did you see?"

She pressed a long finger to her bottom lip before running the same finger down the path of her scar. Her gaze drifted to a point well beyond his shoulder, but he didn't look away from her face. "It was so dark in that room. But he walked past the door as my guard—the one who dropped the map—stepped inside. I could only see a bit of his arm. His sleeves were rolled up past his elbows."

He leaned forward, closing the distance he'd been so eager to find just moments before. "Any distinguishing marks or tattoos?"

"There was something on his arm. A tattoo, maybe."

"Could you draw it?"

"No. It didn't really make any sense. Just oddly put together lines, but it was green, like a classic tattoo on a tan arm."

"Was he hairy?"

She closed her eyes for a long moment, her eyelids dancing. Wrinkles across her forehead and the thin line of her lips reminded him that this was not a pleasant memory for her. And he hated that he was the one asking her to relive it.

But if they could just identify the American and stop his plot, she'd be free to live the life she should have.

"Not particularly. But the hair he had was dark."

"So, we're looking for a man with an unidentified tattoo, dark hair and an American accent."

Shrugging, she nodded. "Not much to go on, I know. But if I could just hear him speak, I think I'd be able to point him out."

"And if you get that close, you'd also be in even more danger than you are now." His tone took on a low growl, and he cleared his throat, trying to get rid of it. He didn't need to have any kind of reaction to this woman. But the protective instincts she brought to the surface were anything but unaffected.

He rubbed a hand over his churning stomach, catching a finger in the belt loop of his BDU pants.

He needed to do something with this girl, but what? She was in trouble, and he wouldn't leave her to fend for herself. No matter what protocol dictated.

"I can stay here." She straightened her spine and ran her hands down the side of her black stretch pants. "I'll be okay. And I'll be able to keep an eye out for anyone snooping around."

"That's what I'm afraid of."

Her face turned into a mask of confusion at his words.

"If you stay put, someone just might snoop around and find you. And then where would you end up?"

Her eyes grew wide, her mouth forming a perfect O. A faint quiver in her bottom lip exposed her fear before she could clamp her straight white teeth on it.

She was scared. And for good reason. If she was found, she could end up back in a room just like her Lybanian cell. Or worse. And he couldn't come rushing in to rescue her again. But he could keep her from ending up in that same spot. Maybe it was just an extension of the mission, but something deep in his gut told him that she needed his protection. Not just anyone would do. She needed him.

Sure, it was against regulations. And he knew firsthand the pain that came with getting too emotionally involved with a woman who didn't understand how little he had to give as a SEAL.

But she didn't need just anyone. She needed *him*.

The knot in his stomach pulled taut.

The road down which his mind wandered was fraught with landmines. This was a bad idea. He'd failed when another pretty face had needed a protector.

Maybe this time would be different. Maybe this time he could save her.

Staci batted long lashes at him. Not flirting, really. Just graceful movements that shaded her eyes. The fear there flickered as she dropped her gaze toward her folded hands, her shoulders sloping as she looked away.

He didn't have to do much. Just had to stay by her side, keep her close and in his line of sight. Who could blame him for taking care of an innocent in danger?

And if she developed feelings or wanted more than just his help?

He shoved the thought away.

Staci just wanted to be safe. And if she indicated she wanted more than that from him? He could gently remind her that she was probably just feeling residual emotions from the prison rescue. He wasn't the settling-down type. There were better men for that.

There was only one way to keep her safe until they figured out who was behind this.

"My sister is staying with me right now, but I've got an extra room at my place. Why don't you stay with us?"

FIVE

The only thing more surprising than L.T.'s blurted question was her immediate response.

"All right." Staci pressed her hands down her pant legs as her own words ran on the tail of his question. "I'd hate to be extra trouble."

He shook his head, the emotions on his face not quite matching his invitation. "My sister, Ashley, is about your age, and her husband is in training in Chicago for a couple more weeks. She could use the company—and the distraction. She's at my place in case she goes into labor early."

Staci pressed a flat hand against her mouth. "Labor?"

"Yes. She's expecting my first nephew in about a month."

Her stomach flipped and turned. Why had she been so quick to agree to stay with them? Sure, she wasn't safe in her own home, but that might be preferable to sharing a roof with a pregnant woman her own age.

It had been easier seeing expectant mothers around town and at church from a distance. Easier still in Lybania, where burkas covered baby bumps at every stage until mothers couldn't leave their homes. No reminders of what would never be.

But every day in a house with a woman who would

clearly be showing, clearly be nesting for her little one's arrival?

That had disaster written all over it.

"You want to pack up a bag, and I'll take you there now?"

"Umm…" She swung her head around the room, her heart picking up speed as she searched for an excuse, a reason to back out of their too-hasty agreement.

L.T. squinted at her, his nostrils flaring just enough to tell her he'd noticed her hesitation.

"I was just thinking… That is… Maybe I should see about…" She squeezed her fingers into a fist and took a deep breath. "Maybe a hotel would be better. Yes. I could get a hotel room."

If it was possible, his eyes narrowed even farther and he pressed his hands onto his hips. "A hotel room is hard to secure—it's too easy for anyone to just walk in from the street. You'll be safer at my place." The tone of his voice was just like one he'd used with his team during her rescue. "And you'll like my sister. Everyone does."

She blinked rapidly, taking a quick step away from him. "I'm sure she's great, but I hate to intrude. She's probably—"

"She's going crazy spending so much time alone when I'm on the base. And the doctor told her she had to cut back her hours at work, so she could really use someone to talk to."

Great. Now he'd cornered her so that if she backed out, she'd look as though she didn't care about her own safety *and* that she didn't care about a pregnant woman.

It wasn't that she wasn't interested in befriending his sister. Ashley was probably a lovely woman.

But watching a pregnancy in full bloom? Could anything dredge up more memories or remind her more fully of her own deficiencies?

Staci attempted a smile at the same time that L.T. glanced over his shoulder—probably wondering what kind of trouble his men could be getting into on the other side of the front door. "I appreciate the invitation. But maybe it would be better for me to stay here. I could be some sort of…bait."

He shook his head and crossed his arms over the expanse of his chest. "There's no need for that." His voice dipped low, brooking no argument. "You'll be safe with us until we can figure out who this guy is and what his plans are."

Just because he didn't want her to counter didn't mean she was going to give in. "I could just as easily run into him while I'm staying with you."

"Yes. And then I'll be by your side. And I'll take care of it."

The muscles in his forearms flexed. Oh, dear. If the sinewy ropes of those arms were any indication, he could handle pretty much anything.

"But you said yourself that you're at the base most of the time. You won't be with me every minute of the day."

His brows knitted together, eyes squinting as he dragged a hand through his hair.

There. He couldn't argue with that. She'd have to be alone sometimes, and that meant that he couldn't always protect her. She might as well stay in her own home, sleep in her own bed and keep her distance from pregnant women.

"No. I won't be with you every second, but at least at my place you won't be alone all of the time. And my guys will pitch in and keep watch on you, too." Staring hard into her eyes, he leaned forward, balancing on one foot and then the other.

He seemed determined, but she went for one last try. "What if this guy waits until you're not around to make another attempt?"

He uncrossed his arms and flexed his hands. "If you're concerned about it, we'll figure something out. Wouldn't you feel better staying with me? You just said yes, didn't you?"

Oh. He'd noticed.

Any chance she could blame her mildly unbalanced behavior on three weeks in a Middle Eastern jail cell? Or a hit-and-run? Or the pipe bomb that his team had rushed out the door?

Her lungs clenched as the reality of all of those surged through her, her knees buckling under their weight.

She didn't need a reminder why she should go with him.

Her options were limited. Go with him and stay out of the lunatic's line of fire. Or avoid the very pregnant lady and leave herself in the crosshairs of a madman.

With a measured breath she emptied her lungs. Wrapping her arms around her waist, she nodded slowly.

"I suppose you're right."

"Fair enough." He didn't look particularly happy about being right, but his voice wasn't unkind. "You want to pack a bag? I'll clean up in here, then take you to my place and drop you off with Ashley."

She did as he suggested, shoving jeans and a few tops into her suitcase. She yanked a skirt and sweater set—interview clothes—out of the closet, rolling them into balls before slipping them into the case. On top she threw in her makeup case, hair dryer and her oversized Chargers jersey. Even if she couldn't be in her own home, she could feel like it with the football shirt her dad had given her before she left for Lybania. Somehow it helped thinking he was near.

Even if he had no idea what was going on.

If she told her parents, they'd insist she stay with them until the risk was past. But that just left them as vulnerable as she was.

She'd meant what she'd said to L.T. earlier. She wasn't going to put her sister or her parents in jeopardy. And that meant biting her tongue when they called.

As she slipped a light jacket over a fresh shirt and pair of jeans, L.T. thumped twice on the door of her room. "You about ready?"

She opened it. "I guess."

He reached around her for the handle of her bag, holding it as if its weight didn't even register on his internal scale. Leading the way to the door, he glanced over his shoulder as she grabbed her glasses and toothbrush from the bathroom.

She spun in a slow circle, taking quick inventory of anything she might be missing. Clothes. Check. Makeup. Check. Bills?

"Who's going to check my mail?"

He lifted a shoulder. "We're going to be less than ten miles away. We can check in every now and then. With any luck we'll find the guy in just a few days, so you won't miss anything important."

A few days? All of this could be over so soon? She was scared to hope for it, but couldn't deny the relief that the idea brought. To be free from this storm would mean she could start her life again. She could figure out her next move and find a new purpose.

She nodded quickly before following him out the door and turning the dead bolt into place with a solid click. Dropping the keys into her purse, she turned toward the two trucks parked at her curb. It was amazing that none of her neighbors had made a commotion about the 4x4s taking up most of the narrow street. Then again, maybe the other residents had gotten a look at the men leaning against the pickups and didn't want to have to face them.

Three SEALs pushed themselves off the side of the first truck, standing at easy attention. They didn't twitch or tremble, their arms hanging loosely at their sides.

Immediately the side of her face itched, and she fought the urge to run a finger down her scar. She didn't have to flit around just because their inherent stillness made her skin tingle. Even if it really wasn't natural to be so motionless.

Or maybe she still clung to every motion as a reminder of her own humanity.

The youngest guy—the one L.T. had called Willie—followed her with his eyes, then settled them onto his lieutenant.

"I'm going to take her home, and then I'll meet you all back at the base."

Willie's eyebrows rose in the silent question that loomed over all of them. Wasn't this her home?

Without pretense or preamble L.T. said, "She's going to stay with me and Ashley for a bit."

Zig lifted one brown eyebrow, but they all remained silent.

And somehow it was worse than if they'd teased or joked about it. What did they think of her?

"She's still the mission until she's completely safe. And we're all going to pitch in." L.T. stared at each of his men, daring them to question his command. "Understood?"

The steel in his voice sent a shiver down her back, and she zipped her coat all the way to her chin. The men, on the other hand, weren't intimidated. They simply nodded their agreement and mumbled a few "yes, sirs" before piling into the first truck and leaving her standing alone beside the only man between her and danger.

Tristan hefted Staci's bag from the bed of his truck and carried it toward his front door just as Ashley stepped onto the stoop. With both hands on her back, round belly sticking out, she filled the space between the door jambs. When she spotted Staci, Ashley's eyes lit up, a smile breaking through her tense expression. She tried to hide her discomfort, but he'd noticed the lines around her mouth and wrinkled forehead when she thought he wasn't looking. Carrying a baby was hard work, and anything that took her mind off it was a treat.

Especially without her husband by her side during the past month.

Maybe Staci would be a good diversion.

"Who's this?" Ashley's voice carried across the lawn, her hips swaying gently, her weight shifting from one foot to the other.

Staci tugged on one of her curls and offered a reserved smile, the warmth he'd known in her eyes all but gone, replaced with a hesitancy he'd never seen her show before.

"Ash, this is my friend, Staci."

His sister's eyes narrowed and then grew wide, recognition washing over her face. He hadn't told Ashley what he and her husband, Matt, had been up to the month before. Not a word about the mission. But Staci's face had been plastered all over the news networks and papers.

As Staci reached the turn in the flat walkway, Ashley swung the front door wide. "Come on into my igloo."

The fans on constant rotation in the living room blew Staci's long hair around her head, and she wrestled it into place, turning slowly around the room.

Compared to her pristine white floors and walls, his place had to look like the epitome of the man cave. Big-screen TV, brown leather couches and a recliner with his form clearly imprinted into it.

Of course, there were no empty cans or crumbs littering the room. Not even before Ashley arrived.

A clean space connoted discipline. And he knew a thing or two about that.

Ash closed the door behind them, her gaze never leaving Staci's face. "I'm Ashley Waterstone. I'm so happy to know you."

Staci managed a ginger smile in response. "Staci Hayes."

"Yes. I've seen your picture in the newspaper. You've had a rough couple months, haven't you?" Ash didn't wait for Staci's response before plowing on. "How'd you meet Tristan?"

From his stance behind Ashley, he caught Staci's gaze, which was filled with questions. Was it okay to say how they'd met? Should she keep the danger she was in a secret?

But he didn't have to respond.

Ashley whipped her head around so fast she nearly threw herself off balance and had to grab his arm for stability. When her feet were firmly beneath her, she glared at him hard. "Matt said you went on a training mission. He said it wasn't anything to worry about. He said you'd barely left the country."

Tristan looked to the ceiling and searched for an answer that wouldn't raise her blood pressure any more than it already was. And wouldn't land him or his best friend in hotter water. He hadn't considered this repercussion of bringing Staci home. Of course Ashley had put two and two together. "Matt's a good husband. He was just looking out for you and the baby. He didn't want to worry you."

Just like Tristan wasn't going to worry her with the details of the threat against Staci.

Her eyes narrowed and she leaned toward him. "Where is Matt right now?"

Tristan chuckled, lifting up the hand that wasn't holding the suitcase. "Right where he said. He's in Chicago doing demo training."

Finally the muscles in her face relaxed and she turned around—slower and more in control than before—and nodded slowly at Staci, whose eyes were bright with concern and confusion.

"I'm sorry about that," Ash said. "My husband told me he was going on a last-minute training mission about four weeks ago. But clearly he was with my brother, and I assume you, too. But I'm just glad you're all safe now."

Staci blinked twice, her mouth hanging open.

"You met Matt for a minute," Tristan explained. "He's the senior chief."

She lifted a hand above her head. "The really tall one?"

Ash nodded. "Yes. That's him." A tender smile broke through her frown. She never could stay mad at Matt. "Well, it's very nice to meet you, Staci. I'm glad you're safe. I know firsthand how good these guys are."

The memory his sister alluded to hit him like a punch to the gut, stealing his breath. Yet another time his work as a SEAL meant he hadn't been there to protect someone he loved. He was just thankful that recovery from an injury had meant that Matt was still stateside at the time, and that he'd been able to keep Ashley safe. And, incidentally, fall in love with her.

"Firsthand?"

With a flippant wave of her hand—like her kidnapping

and capture by a man with no respect for life hadn't taken years off her brother's and husband's lives—Ash smiled. "Oh, sometime I'll tell you about it. But right now, I'm starving. Are you hungry? It's time for my second breakfast."

"Second breakfast?" Staci's head tilted to the side.

Ashley laughed. "Like every pregnant woman, one breakfast simply won't do. It's only fair, really, I *am* eating for two—each of us should get our own meal." Without hesitation she ushered her guest into the kitchen and began pulling leftovers from the fridge. Homemade pizza and lasagna. Apples and peanut butter. Blueberries and yogurt.

She may not have been the one keeping his house clean, but his refrigerator had never been so well stocked. Even if she sometimes mixed her foods into the strangest concoctions he'd ever seen.

Ever the hostess, Ash pointed toward one of the tall stools at the countertop. "Why don't you take a seat, and you can fix yourself a plate while Tristan takes your bag to the spare room?"

Staci caught his gaze, and he offered a quick smile that he hoped reassured her before following his sister's orders. Matt had made him promise not to argue with his sister. *Don't let her blood pressure go up. It's not good for her or the baby. Keep her stress low and the baby cooking until I get back,* Matt had said just before thumping Tristan on the shoulder and boarding a transport for the exclusive demolition and explosives training.

He dropped Staci's bag in the room on the second floor next to Ashley's and bounded down the stairwell.

He'd run down another set of stairs just two weeks before. Only that time there had been another hand clutched in his.

He stared at his tingling palm, all the memories from

the night of the rescue racing through his mind. Staci had clung to him, holding on for everything she was worth, following his instructions without complaint. Even when he'd swung her up to his shoulder, she hadn't fought him. And he knew how uncomfortable that position was.

And then she'd tracked him down. She'd gone around every roadblock until she'd found the help that she needed.

The girl sure had some spunk, and his smile grew wider.

As he reached the last step, he paused before walking into the kitchen.

Ashley's voice carried to him without pause. "How's your apple?"

"Very good. Thank you."

"You're quite welcome." A smile laced Ash's voice. He'd heard it before, every time she talked with one of the women at the battered women's shelter where she worked. "May I ask how you ended up in Lybania?"

Staci cleared her throat, and it sounded like she picked up a cup and plunked it back on the counter before responding. "A couple from my church, Judy and Hank, had been over there doing medical care, and they spoke one Sunday about the work they were doing, helping kids get the education, care and love they needed."

There was a long pause, and he leaned against the wall, holding his breath, hoping she would go on.

She did. "My boyfr—" Her voice broke and she cleared her throat before taking her story in a different direction. "My life was in flux. I thought I had a plan, but it didn't work out. I wasn't really sure what was next, but when I heard Judy and Hank talk about the kids, I thought I might be able to help. I was an elementary ed major in college, so I figured I could teach some English and just be there for the kids. At least do something."

"And then what happened?"

"I was there for two years without a problem. We offered free low-level medical care—Hank was a nurse—to women and children in need. And in Lybania that's just about everyone. We gave out food and offered classes for the women, teaching them skills that they could use to help support their families.

"And then police came." Her voice took on a distant quality, as though she was more in the Middle East than Southern California. "They had guns like I'd never seen. Big and black and ugly. Hank had a line of patients waiting to see him, but the gunmen just barged in, herding us into a rickety, brown van.

"There had been a dust storm that morning, and the air was still thick with it. I thought it was the dirt that made it hard to breathe, but then I realized that my heart was pounding so hard I could feel nothing but the thudding inside my own chest. And my lungs couldn't get enough oxygen."

"I'm so sorry. That must have been terrifying."

Another long pause, and he had to force himself to let out a measured breath and inhale again silently. He shouldn't be listening to this conversation, but he didn't want to interrupt and risk her stopping. This was so different from the briefing he'd received.

The facts were the same. But the details made the story real.

This was her life before he'd met her. Before he'd stolen her from under the noses of those madmen.

"I'm glad I couldn't hear anything else, because I knew the men were yelling, but I couldn't understand any of their words. Even when the uniformed officers passed us over to the guerrillas, I followed their pointing fingers and angry shoves more than their words. Because whatever they were saying, their tone conveyed the truth. They hated us."

"But why?"

Did she even know why she'd been captured? Did she even know what her crime had been?

"We had a bible."

It sounded like Ashley patted Staci's hand, and his sister sighed. "Did they hurt you?"

Another long pause, and he could envision those long, slender fingers brushing past the scar on her face. "They intended to. But they were waiting for their leader to arrive." Staci's voice tapered off like the wind had carried it away. "And then L.T. showed up. And your husband. And they ran with me until I was on the boat."

"Safe."

Staci made a vague sound that could have been an agreement, but he knew it wasn't.

"Well, I'm—" Ashley grunted. "Oh! This baby is ready to kick his way out."

"He's kicking?"

"He sure is. Want to feel it?"

Staci's stool scraped across the floor, and he assumed she was reaching for Ash's belly until she spoke. "No. That's all right." A short pause and then, "Maybe I should go."

"Where? I mean, if Tristan brought you here, he must think it's the best place for you to stay. You're welcome here."

"I— Thank you. I appreciate it, but with your baby on the way, I don't want to—that is—I don't want to get in your way." Staci's words were a deluge, stammered out fast. But they didn't make any sense.

Why would she want to leave?

"I'd like you to stay." The tone in Ash's voice rang true, compassion woven through every word. "I could use the company if you don't mind."

"But you just met me. You don't even know me."

What had her scared enough that she'd rather face a man trying to kill her than stay in his home?

Whatever it was, he wasn't going to let Staci put herself in danger while he figured it out. They had a bigger problem to deal with. They had to stop a possible terrorist attack.

SIX

The next morning Staci rolled over amid sheets that smelled of fresh mountain streams, the covers wrapping her in a cocoon. Snuggling deeper into the warmth, she squinted at the alarm clock sitting on the nightstand, but she couldn't make out the big red numbers without her glasses. And she couldn't get to them without dislodging her covers.

The sun had only just broken the horizon, its rays reaching through the window to greet her. She'd heard Ashley get up to use the restroom twice during the night, but now all was silent in Tristan's house.

She wasn't quite sure when she'd begun thinking of him as Tristan. It was probably during Ashley's fervent appeal for her to stay. Over and over Ashley had pointed at her big brother and called him by name.

Now Staci was calling him Tristan and staying under his roof.

She'd had her chance to get away from the constant reminder of her own inadequacy, to leave before she became attached to Ashley and the baby she carried.

But she'd given in and stayed. And now it was too late.

She already adored the waddling woman, whose gentle words and kind smile had prompted Staci to share more about the ordeal than she'd even shared with the PAO at the base. The only person she'd told more to was Tristan. And that was so she could show him the map.

When he'd rounded the corner into the kitchen the day before, he'd immediately made it clear that she wasn't going anywhere. This was the safest place for her to be.

Even if watching a joyfully rotund Ashley navigate the last weeks of her pregnancy made Staci's chest hurt.

She rubbed a flat palm across her collarbone, wishing the air would come a little easier.

But the sure knowledge that she'd never get to have a child of her own ripped at her heart.

The hardest part was the certainty that no man would ever want to marry her for that very reason.

Chris had been clear when he broke off their relationship. Silly her, she'd thought he was going to propose.

I've been thinking a lot about us, Stace.

Me, too. She'd smiled and held out her hand over the linen tablecloth, expecting him to take it. He hadn't.

There's not really a future for us, is there?

Her mouth had dropped open, a bite of prime rib sticking in her throat as she grabbed for her water glass. She'd gulped as tears flooded her eyes.

When her glass had rattled back on the table, she'd tried to speak, but the words had lodged somewhere behind her tongue.

Listen, it's better to talk about this now, right? Before we got serious.

Serious? she'd croaked. *We've been together for more than a year. I moved to San Diego so that we could live in the same city.*

He hadn't even had the courtesy to apologize for leading her on, but his ears had turned pink and he'd looked away, unable to hold her gaze. *I never asked you to. And you weren't really honest with me about everything back then, were you?*

The flames behind her eyes had flickered to life, setting her temples on fire. *I wasn't honest with you?*

You never told me about—about your situation. You know I want to have a family.

So do I. There are other options like foster care or adoption.

When he'd finally swung his stare back to her, his eyes had been hard and cold, and he'd wiped the tip of a cloth napkin across his mouth. *I want a family of my own kids.*

There's surrogacy—we can figure something out. If we love each other there must be a way.

He'd pulled out his wallet and dug out a couple of bills, shaking his head the whole time.

Please. Please don't leave. Don't throw everything away because of this. Her voice had risen on the last word, desperation filling her.

She'd been shocked to realize she was nearly begging him to stay. That wasn't who she was. She was stronger than that. She was strong at twenty-one when the OB/GYN told her that the ovarian tumors would have to be removed, and with them any hope of ever bearing children. She was strong at twenty-three when she'd watched her little sister get married before her.

But these words from the man who had professed his love had torn through her, taking all her strength away.

He'd stood, brushing his tie smooth and nodding toward the money he'd left on the table. *That should cover the meal.* Then, sticking his hands into his pockets, he'd shrugged. *It's been fun, Stace, but I'm ready to settle down and start a family.*

How had she ever thought Chris could be her lifelong

partner? The cool glint in his eye, the lack of any concern for her, had left her alone and adrift.

And certain of only one thing.

She wasn't whole enough to be wanted.

Ashley's door creaked open just a moment before two quick raps landed on Staci's.

"Staci? Are you awake?"

The insistent whisper launched Staci out of bed, fighting the covers that refused to let her free. Her foot thumped hard on the floor as she tumbled toward the door. Swinging it open, she revealed Ashley wrapped in a cozy robe.

"Is everything all right?" Staci kept her voice low, just as Ashley had.

"Yes. Everything's fine. I just was wondering if you could do me a favor."

Staci let out the breath that she'd been holding. "Oh. Sure. What is it?"

Ashley's smile turned sheepish. "I don't fit behind a steering wheel very well these days." She rubbed a slow hand around her stomach. "And I just got a call that the shelter where I work needs some extra help today. Would you mind taking me?"

That wasn't a good idea. Who knew what was waiting for her beyond the security of these walls? When or where would she have to face the man who was trying to kill her? "What about your brother? What did he say?"

"Oh, Tristan's been gone for hours. He does PT with the rest of the team most mornings."

He'd said she'd be safe here. Said that here she didn't need to worry about the American they needed to identify. That's why she'd agreed to stay, despite the knot that Ashley's pregnancy left in her stomach.

Staying kept her safe and gave them the best shot at identifying the man and his plan.

But what about leaving the house with Ashley?

Ashley ran a hand over her hair. "It would only be for the morning." She raised her eyebrows, showing off her big blue eyes. She looked like she was trying to be the picture of sweetness, but there was a wry humor to her eyes that never quite vanished. "Please. I'll buy you lunch. Anything that ten bucks can buy is yours."

The knot in her stomach loosened as a little chuckle escaped. "But I don't have my car here. It's still in the shop."

"We can take mine." Ashley's smile said she knew Staci would cave.

And she was right. Staci couldn't leave Ashley without a ride or let the women and children at the shelter suffer just because she'd rather not get too close to Ashley.

Or leave the house.

Anyway, the lunatic after her didn't know she was here. He probably thought she was still at her own home, so if she left from here, he couldn't follow her. They'd be fine for the day.

"All right."

Ashley nearly clapped in glee. "Wonderful. Let's leave in an hour." She winked. "It takes me a little longer to get ready these days."

Staci closed her door and leaned her head back against the wall. It would never take her longer to get ready because of a baby on board. Maybe that was something to be thankful for.

"Oh, God, please help me to be thankful for what I do have. I'm healthy now, and I have a loving family. And Tristan will keep me as safe as possible for now."

Her prayer helped but didn't fully brighten her mood as she moved around the room, picking out clothes and necessities before slipping into the bathroom across the hall to get ready.

An hour later it was Ashley's smile and laughter as they drove to the battered women's shelter that pulled her all the way out of her doldrums.

Ashley waved her hand around the passenger side of the coupe as Staci pulled them onto the interstate. "So then Aubrey had the kite sailing, but Jorge had never flown a kite before. So there he was running and skipping below it, but he didn't know about the string. He ran right into it." Her voice rose with excitement as she retold the story. "And we all started calling out to him to stop and turn, but when he did, the string was stuck to him. Before we knew it, he was so tightly wrapped up that he couldn't even lift his arms."

Staci chuckled at the image of the five-year-old's first experience with a kite.

"How long have you been volunteering at the shelter?"

"Almost two years now. I started helping out right after I moved from Northern California."

Staci shot her a look out of the corner of her eye, wondering if she'd go on. When she didn't, Staci prodded, "What brought you to San Diego?"

Her smile widened, and she spread her fingers over her stomach. "Matt." This time Ashley didn't require any urging to continue. "I was in love with him, and I wasn't going to let him get away even if Tristan wasn't happy that I had plans for his best friend."

"So Matt was your brother's best friend *before* you got married?"

"They were swim buddies during SEAL training more than ten years ago. And they've been best friends ever since. A couple years ago I got into a bit of a mess, and Tristan couldn't check on me, so he sent Matt."

"And you just fell in love?"

"Something like that."

Staci's smile widened. Tristan had to have hated that. He commanded his men with a sure hand and doted on his sister. Combining the two was probably torture on him.

That, more than anything else, tickled her, and she let out a full-body laugh as she pulled off I-5 toward the shelter.

Tristan ran his hands through his damp hair and over his shaved chin as he marched down the single hallway of the mobile office unit. It was good to be clean and in a fresh uniform after a harder than usual PT. He didn't usually lead the group. He had a better view of his team, a better understanding of their skills, when he stuck to the middle of the pack.

But this morning, he'd been so focused on the woman still sleeping under his roof—and the man after her—that he'd run the beach with abandon, leaving most of his men in his wake.

Zig stuck his head out of the door of the office across the hall. "Pushed yourself pretty hard this morning, eh, L.T.?"

"Guess I did." He didn't address the underlying question in Zig's words. He didn't need to explain himself. He was still the leader of his squad, the second in command of the platoon. And if he wanted to run faster than usual, he would.

As he stepped into his tiny office, the phone on his desk rang. Snatching it to his ear, he said, "This is L.T. Sawyer."

"Lieutenant Sawyer. This is Commander Henry Kyle."

"Sir. It's good to hear back from you." Tristan had spent more hours with the commander than anyone else in his time at the academy. Even after graduation, he sought him out as a linguistics mentor. The man was a language genius—hopefully he could help them translate the few words on the little map.

"Sure. I got your email with the scanned page."

Well, it wasn't the whole page. But the commander didn't need to know that he'd removed the map from the image after scanning it. "Great. Do you have any idea what it says? It's a dialect I've never seen."

"Where did you get it?"

"I'm sorry, sir. That's classified."

"Mmm-hmm." The older man mumbled something that sounded like he understood. "Well, without knowing the exact area of origin, based on the tails—and something I saw in the news recently—I'd wager this came from Lybania."

Smart man. Of course he'd put two and two together. But Tristan didn't confirm or deny Kyle's suspicions. "Any idea what it says?"

"I'm pretty sure it says that the second will be first."

"The second will be first?" That wasn't much to go on.

"Yes. But what's strange about it is the word that they use for *second* is actually one that I've only ever seen in intercepted missives from terrorist cells. It means the second in command, the leader's proxy."

Tristan wrote the phrase on a piece of paper, tracing each letter over and over as he turned the phrase around in his mind. "So the second in command is going to become the first in command." He tried to say it with confidence, but it didn't fit into the bigger picture of what he knew, so he stumbled on the last word.

"Could be." Kyle took a long pause. "Or it could be that the second will get something before everyone else."

But what would he get? And who's second? Was a terrorist leader about to send his deputy to blow up something in San Diego? Staci had said she'd heard them talking about an explosive, but how did that, the map and the second all tie together?

"What are you mixed up in, Sawyer?"

The quiet question caught Tristan off guard, but he fought to keep his mind focused. "I'm really not sure, sir. But I'm taking this through the appropriate channels." In fact he had a meeting with the officer who oversaw all of the SEAL teams at Coronado scheduled for that afternoon. Tristan would tell him the truth about what was going on— even about Staci staying at his place—and then they'd make a plan for how to keep her safe and make sure that the terrorist's bomb never struck its mark.

"Be sure you do."

"Yes, sir. Thank you for your help."

He hung up the phone quickly before dialing a new number. "You've reached the office of Special Agent Victor Salano. Leave me a message, and I'll return your call."

"Vic, it's L.T. I've got a translation on the words on that map I sent you." He thought about leaving the translation in the voice mail, but stopped before repeating it. Maybe it would be better to check with Staci to see if she could put it in some kind of context. Maybe the words would jog her memory, and she could shed some light on them.

This was a good excuse to call her, to reassure her that she'd made the right decision to stay. This was also a good excuse just to listen to the sound of her voice—a little husky but still filled with a smile even in the face of this threat.

Except that was not why he was going to call her. This wasn't about her voice or her pretty face or the way she was both confident and vulnerable at the same time. This was about the mission, and nothing more.

He punched his home number into the base of the oversized, outdated office phone. As it rang, he ran his pen over the letters he'd written during his conversation with

Commander Kyle, replaying the commander's words over and over.

The second will be first.

He took the sentence apart, putting the words back together in different structures.

Will the second be first?

The first will be second.

First, the second will be.

What if it wasn't a complete thought at all? What if the words had been transposed in the translation? That wasn't uncommon, and usually easy to figure out in context. But there was no perspective for these words. He could be missing a whole phrase and not even know it.

He was so consumed with scribbling words on his page that he didn't realize he'd missed five rings until his old-fashioned answering machine clicked on.

"Leave a message at the beep."

His stomach churned. Why hadn't Ashley or Staci answered?

Maybe they were waiting to find out who was calling.

After the tone sounded, he said, "Ash? Staci? Are you there? It's Tristan. Pick up." He waited for several long seconds, each tick of the hand on his watch twisting the knot in his stomach a little tighter. "Call me back as soon as you get this."

He slammed the receiver down, pushing his boots against the floor until he sat ramrod-straight in his chair. Grabbing his cell from his bag, he checked for a call or text from his sister.

Nothing.

He hit the button to speed-dial her cell phone, his toe tapping a staccato cadence on the tiled floor. The call went immediately to voice mail, and he ground out a succinct message for her. "Call me back."

Had he made a terrible mistake bringing Staci home? Had she been attacked, and Ashley with her?

He couldn't help but replay the scenes from two years before in his mind. Ashley's interference in a human trafficking ring had led to her being chained up and held in a dank cell. Matt had turned his back for only a moment, and she'd been taken.

What if it had happened again?

He pushed equal parts bile and fear back down his throat and scrolled through his phone to find the number that Staci had given him. It was too soon to think about the worst. Maybe they were just in the backyard.

Pressing the button to call Staci, he took several deep breaths through his nose as it rang and rang, finally clicking over to voice mail. He didn't bother leaving her a message, instead jumping to his feet and racing for the door. As he shoved an arm into the sleeve of his jacket, he stopped short.

Where could he go? Back to his place, maybe?

Where would the girls have gone? If they'd left the house voluntarily, they could have gone shopping or to... the shelter.

He jabbed stiff fingers at the key pad on his phone, praying that the girls would be there.

"Pacific Coast House, this is Dawn. How can I help you?"

"This is Lieutenant Sawyer. I'm looking for my sister, Ashley Waterstone. Is she—"

"Sure thing. Hold on, she's right here."

He pressed a hand to the top of his desk, his elbow locking into place and keeping him from falling over as relief washed through him.

"Tristan?"

He wanted to yell at her for scaring him, but instead he let out a loud sigh.

"What's wrong?" she asked, her voice rising.

Keep her calm. He had to keep her calm. "Everything's fine. I was just trying to get in touch with Staci. Is she with you?"

"Of course. I had her drive me here."

He let out a slow breath between tight lips, rubbing his temples with slow circular motions. Of course. He'd thought about warning Ashley about the danger, letting her know to be on the lookout for anyone suspicious hanging around, but in the end, he'd decided against it. Rock would have his head if he scared or upset Ashley. And anyway, he'd assumed they'd stay in the house, where they'd be safe. He should have known better. Since he hadn't warned Ashley that there could be danger, she'd taken Staci under her wing and into the wide open.

But what could he say to get her to understand that Staci couldn't leave the house without a guard?

A thump at his office door had him looking into the face of Captain Crawford, his executive officer—second in command of the entire naval base at Coronado. He covered the mouthpiece of his phone and straightened up. "Sir?"

"Tomorrow's tactical meeting has been moved to fourteen hundred today."

"Yes, sir."

"Be at my office a half hour early so that we can look at the intel and compare notes."

"Yes, sir."

Crawford stalked away as Tristan lowered himself back into his seat. He wouldn't be able to get away to personally see that Staci got safely back home.

"Tristan?"

"Sorry. My XO just stopped by."

"What did you need?"

His eyes roamed the room, searching for something to remind him why he'd been trying to track them down in the first place. He landed on the notepad by his phone. "Can I talk with Staci?"

"Staci, huh?" That infernal smile filled Ashley's voice. "And just what is it you want to say to her?" She was teasing him as if he were sixteen instead of thirty-three. Actually, she'd been doing that a lot lately, trying to get him to open up about his romantic relationships. Or at least define his relationship with Robin, who he hadn't seen in well over a year. He just couldn't bring himself to tell her that he and Robin had never been serious. He couldn't do serious after losing Phoebe.

Ashley was pushing him to find that special someone.

She just didn't know that he didn't want one.

Well, that wasn't quite true. There was something amazing about the idea of sharing his life with a sweet-smelling, hand-holding, eye-popping woman. He just couldn't be there for her when she really needed him.

And he couldn't live with himself if that happened again.

"Just put her on the phone, would you?"

Ashley laughed. "Fine."

A moment later, Staci's voice, clear and strong, rang through the line. "Hello?"

He scrubbed a hand down his face, the urge to yell at her battling the relief that she was safe. "What were you thinking leaving the house?"

She cleared her throat. "Well, I figured he doesn't know where I'm staying." Her voice dropped to a whisper. "And your sister asked for my help."

"She has no idea what kind of danger you're in."

"At all?"

"None. Stress can raise her blood pressure, which is bad for the baby and bad for her. It could cause her to go into early labor or worse, so I'm trying to keep her calm."

"So you didn't tell her anything?"

He pinched his eyes closed, sinking to his chair and leaning his elbow on the desk. Pressing a finger and thumb against his eyelids, he said, "Well, what should I have told her?"

She was silent for a long time, her even breathing the only thing assuring him that she hadn't hung up.

Shaking his hand and letting the tension fall away, he sighed. "I'm sorry. I just didn't expect you to leave the house this morning. And then I couldn't reach you. Why didn't you answer your phone?"

"I forgot it when we left the house this morning." Her words barely escaped, and the picture of her in his mind was her huddled form in the corner of that dark room in Lybania.

"All right. We'll talk about this tonight. Right now I have to get ready for a meeting. I can't come get you, so I'm going to send one of my guys to make sure you get home safely. All right? I want you to go home and stay at home until I get there. Understood?"

"Fine." Power flickered in her single word, like she wasn't really agreeing to his terms.

"I'm not kidding."

"I know."

She hung up before he could say anything more, and he shouted down through the open door. "Willie G., get in here!"

The kid's heavy footsteps thudded down the hallway, and he appeared, breathless and at attention. "Sir?"

"Whatever is on your schedule this afternoon, cancel it. I have a special assignment for you."

SEVEN

Staci knelt before six-year-old twin sisters, both with their blond hair in pigtails and mouths circled in the remnants of red punch. Studying the papers they held in their hands, she nodded slowly before pointing to one of the drawings. "A purple giraffe, not often seen in nature. Very creative, Zoe."

The little girl giggled as Staci shifted to her sister. "And what do we have here? Is this you and your sister, Tiara?"

"And our mommy."

"What a beautiful family."

The girls laughed, both showing off their missing front teeth and sparkling blue eyes. But when the shelter's front door opened and someone stepped inside, both girls' eyes grew wide with fear.

Staci spun around, keeping herself between the little ones and whatever had scared them.

"Will?" It was easy to see how the broad-shouldered SEAL would frighten Zoe and her sister, even with a genuine smile plastered on his face.

"Ms. Hayes." He tipped the brim of his nonexistent hat.

She rolled her eyes. "I can't be much older than you are. Just call me Staci, please."

"L.T. sent me to make sure you and Mrs. Waterstone make it back home safely."

A tiny hand slipped into hers, and Staci gave it a gentle squeeze before bending over to meet the girl's blue eyes. "Tiara, this is my friend Will. Will, this Tiara and Zoe."

He squatted in front of them, his camouflage pants pulling at the knees as he dug into a side pocket. "I thought I might run into some pretty girls here. So I brought a few treats." He produced a couple colorfully wrapped suckers, holding one in each hand out to the girls.

"Go ahead, girls. It's all right."

Ashley had joined them, her encouragement all that the kids needed. They snatched the lollipops and unwrapped them in a flash before disappearing to the playroom.

"Will, what are you doing here?" Ashley took a deep breath and touched Staci's arm as though using it for support. "Is Matt all right?"

His forehead wrinkled and then returned to normal. "Sure. The senior is just fine. Far as I know."

"And Tristan?"

"L.T.'s fine, too."

"Then what brings you down here?"

"I was in the area, and L.T. asked me to drop by, make sure you two made it home okay."

Staci bit her lip to keep from revealing too much to Ashley, looking at her feet until Will spoke again.

"Are you about ready to go? Or should I come back?"

"Will Gumble, tell me what's going on." With her hands on her hips, feet spread wide, Ashley leaned forward. Despite the concern etched into her words, she looked like a miniature linebacker, ready to face the field of battle.

He swallowed, running a finger around the collar of his T-shirt before shoving his hands into his pockets and looking to Staci for help.

But what was she supposed to say? How could she assure Ashley enough to keep her calm, but give her a valid reason for Will to stay by their sides?

God, give me the words.

"It's my fault." Two sets of eyes, heavy with curiosity, swung toward her. She tried for a smile, but only produced about half of one. "I was in a car accident recently, and I guess your brother is worried that I might not get you safely home. He sent Will here to make sure that we make it back to the house safely this afternoon."

Will nodded his agreement with the story.

"That's ridiculous." Then Ashley sighed like a sister used to putting up with her brother's overprotective ways. "Fine. I'm almost ready to go."

She walked to the shelter's front desk, which sat in the line of sun coming through the windows on either side of the front door. Speaking quietly with Mildred, the shelter director, and the office administrator, Ashley pressed her fists into the small of her back, as though the extra weight she carried made her ache all over.

"Thank you for coming," Staci said, keeping her voice low enough that it would just reach the man standing beside her.

"L.T. says you're in a bit of trouble. I'm happy to help."

"Were you there?" His eyebrows knit together in confusion. "In Lybania?" she clarified. "Were you there that night?"

He didn't say anything for a long time. And then very quietly, "Yes, ma'am. I was with Mrs. Timmons."

Her chest tightened at the memory, emotions still so close to the surface that she barely managed to squeak out another word. "Thank you for that, too." The lean man with ruffled brown hair couldn't have been any older than her, but he'd been instrumental in rescuing two of her favorite people in the world. She had a sudden urge to hug him.

Ashley turned back to them, just in time to stop Staci from making the gesture, her voice singing through the big house's entryway. "Ready to go?"

"Hope to see you again, Staci," Mildred said.

She hoped so, too. "It was nice to meet you all."

Will held the door open, and they stepped into the San Diego sunshine, which made the uncovered skin at her neck and forearms tingle. She stopped on the sidewalk in front of the shelter, staring up at the sky and letting the sun warm her face.

An engine revved somewhere down the street, but no car passed by them. Will, too, perked up at the sound, looking over the tops of the cars parked along the narrow residential road. She caught his eye, and he shrugged, shaking his head.

She tried to tell the knot in her stomach that if the SEAL wasn't concerned, she didn't need to be either. But here in the open, she couldn't help but feel exposed, visible to the whole world.

Exposed for a particular American man to find.

"We parked across the street." She pointed to Ashley's car, which hadn't seemed far from the shelter that morning. Now it felt like a football field away when she thought about the man after her.

Biting her lip if only to have something to focus on other than the tremors in her hands and wayward direction of her thoughts, she took a step toward the car.

The man looking for her didn't know that she was staying with the Sawyers. He couldn't know that she'd been at *this* shelter today.

The unseen car revved its engine again, and her heart jumped into her throat, but she pushed forward.

Ashley followed her between two parked SUVs, and just before Staci stepped into the open street, Will slipped between the two women. She turned to glance into his eyes. He wasn't as tall as Tristan, but his shoulders were just as steady as she took the last step into the unprotected road.

Nothing happened. No careening car or sniper bullets.

She let out a wavering breath on a laugh. How silly to work herself into such a frenzy over nothing. She was safe. Taking a second step, the tension in her neck drained away, and she managed a quick grin back at Will, who held his arm out for Ashley.

But as Staci took a third step, tires at the end of the road shrieked against the pavement, the smell of burning rubber already assaulting her nose.

She froze in the middle of the road, her muscles refusing to move.

Just move. She had to move.

But she couldn't.

A white van—just like the one that had run her off the road four days before—barreled down on her, and she was helpless.

What had started six weeks before was about to end. The man was going to find his mark.

Suddenly Will shouted. "Stay put." He held up his hands to Ashley, motioning for her to remain between the two parked trucks. And then he slammed into Staci, the momentum of his body carrying her across the rest of the street and into a BMW with a car alarm that immediately hissed and honked its displeasure.

Wrapped in Will's embrace and tucked against the front of him, Staci couldn't even see the van that thundered past them, almost as loud as her heart.

She gasped and grappled at the front of his shirt, looking for some purchase, some way to catch her balance as her head spun around and around.

He stepped away too quickly, holding her up only by her shoulders.

Tristan would have kept her in his arms until the world righted itself. Until she wasn't consumed by the shaking in her legs or the lack of oxygen in her lungs.

"Are you all right?" Will shook her gently, his fingers wrapped around her arms. "Talk to me, Ms. Hayes."

She blinked away the pain thrumming through her head and rubbed her backside where she'd collided with the car. "Call me Staci."

A slow smile crept over his face. "Good. What day is it?"

"A rotten one."

"Close enough."

Just then Ashley's winded breaths reached her side. With soft hands, Ashley rubbed Staci's wrist. "Are you all right? That van almost hit you."

"Yes." Ashley was free to take that in response to either her question or her statement.

The good Lord knew that Staci was well aware of what had almost happened.

"And the white van didn't even slow down. It was like the driver was *trying* to hit her."

Tristan stared across the living room at Staci, whose jean-clad legs were pulled all the way under her chin as she rocked gently on one of his couches, while Ashley all but acted out that afternoon's events.

"You have to do something."

"I will." At his words, Staci looked up from where her forehead had been resting on her knees. He gave her a re-assuring nod, but she still looked paler than a sheet. "Why don't you get ready for bed, Ash? You've been yawning for the last twenty minutes."

His sister eyed them both before accepting his hand to help her out of the recliner. In a hushed tone, she said, "If he hadn't wrapped his arms around her and held her against that other car, I think she would have been hit."

The air left his lungs. It should have been him. He should have been the one to protect Staci, to wrap her in his arms, to comfort her until she stopped shaking.

Instead he'd heard it all second-hand. First from a steely-eyed Willie G. and then from his frantic sister. Patting her arm, he said, "It's going to be all right. I'll take care of it. I promise. Now try to calm down and get some rest."

She nodded before giving Staci a quick hug and then disappearing up the stairs.

Tristan stood over Staci, his hands on his hips. She looked up from where her chin still rested on her knees, her head tilted all the way back. "I'm sorry. I didn't think he'd know I was here. Or there. I didn't mean to put Ashley in danger."

He scrubbed a hand over his face then through his hair, a sigh escaping from somewhere deep. Here he was feeling like a failure, and she felt the same way. They were some team.

Falling to the couch beside her, he put his arm around her shoulders and, as if they'd done this a thousand times, she turned into his embrace. Her head fell to the hollow where his neck and shoulder met, fitting there like he'd been designed for just that purpose.

Her hair smelled of tropical fruit, and he breathed her in. Her slender shoulders trembled in his embrace, and once again, he felt her fear, knew her terror.

But he couldn't stop it.

At least not yet.

"Do you want to talk about it?" Anything to keep her tears at bay.

She shook her head, curling even further into his arms until her head lay against his throat. His pulse picked up.

He hadn't held a woman like this in a long time. It'd been at least four years. Probably a whole lot longer than that. He'd never done this with Robin, who he'd seen on and off for a year. She wasn't big into open displays of affection, which was good for him because he much preferred keeping his distance.

If she didn't get close, he couldn't let her down.

If she never relied on him, he couldn't fail to be there for her.

He'd made this mistake before Robin, with Phoebe. And he wouldn't do it again.

Staci sniffed, and he leaned back, hooking a finger under her chin. She kept her eyelids down, but there were no tears clinging to her long lashes. And the tip of her nose wasn't red.

She hadn't broken down yet.

"I got a call today from one of my linguistics instructors at Annapolis."

Her eyes flew open so that her lashes mingled with the long bangs hanging over her forehead, and he battled the desire to brush them out of her way. "What did he say?"

"He thinks he translated the words on the map." With the hand not holding her close, he reached into the cargo pocket of his pants and pulled out the page of scribbled notes. "I was hoping you might be able to give it some context."

She grabbed for the page. Holding it beneath her nose, her eyes roved back and forth under tense eyebrows. After several long seconds, she shook her head and looked back up to meet his gaze. "The second will be first?"

"If I say that the word translated as second is usually used to connote the second in command, does that help?"

Closing her eyes, she mumbled the phrase over and over. "What about the first? Does that mean the leader or just the first in a series?"

"That's not clear."

She stretched her legs out and rolled out of his hold, which left him with an odd feeling of emptiness. He tried not to focus on it, instead watching her face work through the words and follow his line of thinking as he'd rearranged the words. "You think it might be missing a line?"

He chewed on his bottom lip. "Maybe."

She nodded, talking it through. "But the paper wasn't torn, so if that's true then it would've had to have been left only half-written when it was given to the man who came into my cell."

"Unless he wrote it, and hadn't had a chance to finish."

Her lips puckered in thought and she scratched at the scar in front of her ear. "And is it saying that the second will be the target of the attack? Or that it's just somehow tied to him?"

"Okay, let's say it is complete and that the deputy is the one who's going to be attacked. Who could it be referring to?"

She ran her tongue over her teeth before spitting out ideas as they seemed to come to her. "The deputy mayor? The second in command at Coronado?"

Crawford. He'd just spent all afternoon with the guy. The captain wasn't his favorite, but he was a smart man and an accomplished sailor. And he sure didn't deserve to be the target of whatever was going to go down.

"The vice president?" She blinked after the words popped out, as though she wasn't quite sure where they'd come from. "It couldn't go that high, could it?"

His legs twitched, and he pushed himself off the couch to pace the width of the room. Head bowed and hands clasped behind his back, he stalked from wall to wall, hoping for a bolt of inspiration. An answer to at least one of their many questions.

Without stopping he glanced at her, her head still bent over the paper with the translation written on it.

"It's not safe for you out there." She glanced up but didn't speak. "I mean, after what happened today and not knowing how far or deep this thing goes."

"You're right."

He opened his mouth to argue his point, but stopped short. She'd agreed with him. Of course she had. He was right.

"But I can't stay locked up in this house. Refusing to leave here isn't going to do anything but make Ashley curious why I never go out. Not to mention, I can't help you identify this guy if I'm stuck here."

She was right.

He let out a hard breath through his nose.

He didn't have to like that she was right. He just had to figure out how to keep her safe. Hiding her away on the base wasn't going to do it. He needed a practical way to protect her.

"To start with, you're not going to go anywhere without telling me where you're headed."

She looked about ready to argue that she wasn't sixteen, but instead lowered and lifted her lashes over those giant green eyes, which made her look about that old.

"Second, I'm going to be by your side as much as I can." He marched some more, stamping away the feather-light flicker in his chest that suggested he might like being by her side for more than just her protection. "And if I can't be with you, I'll find someone who can be."

"That's not practical, and you know it. Ashley is going to know something's off if you quit going to work and start sending SEALs by every day."

"I don't care." But he did care.

If he had only Ashley to worry about, he'd have already told her. On any normal day, she could handle the danger with practicality and calm. Her years of working for battered women's shelters meant she was accustomed to dealing with women hiding from dangerous men. But at the moment she carried the most precious cargo in the world, and her emotions were already pulled taut in Matt's absence.

Standing in the middle of the room, he stared at Staci. She didn't blink or look away. She'd survived a Middle Eastern jail cell, a bullet wound and nearly being blown up. She looked small, but she was tough. Tougher than maybe he'd given her credit for.

They stared each other down in silence until he finally said. "Okay. Since I can't be with you every minute until we catch this guy, tomorrow we start training."

"For what?"

"Self-defense."

EIGHT

Staci pulled on the hem of her yellow tank top, wishing for all the world that it would stay a little lower over her hips. Not that she wasn't fully covered. Her black knit workout pants, tennis shoes and top were completely appropriate.

Except that she was going to have to get into close quarters with Tristan.

In that moment, a burka wouldn't have covered enough.

He led the way into a large workout room at the private gym close to his house. He'd said that lots of sailors used these facilities in the early mornings, but by the late morning, they were nearly deserted.

Free weights and machines lined all of the walls except for the corner, which boasted a thick blue mat about the size of the bedroom she was staying in. The adjacent walls were also covered in the padding. Just off the blue pad, a punching bag still swayed where a guy not much bigger than her unwound thick tape from his fists.

Was she really up for this?

Tristan dropped his bag on the wooden floor off the mat and started stretching.

"Want to loosen up?"

She set her bag on the floor next to his and followed him into the center of the mat.

The boxer eyed her as he tucked his gloves into his bag, and she tugged on the edge of her shirt again, looking to Tristan for some sort of encouragement.

As if he could read her mind, he stepped in front of her, blocking the man's view. And hers.

He gave her a soft smile as he approached. "We're going to take it easy today, all right?"

She nodded.

"Do you have any training in self-defense?"

"No."

His smile grew wide. "No wonder you look like a palm tree in Alaska."

"Hey. What's that supposed to mean?"

He lifted both shoulders, stretching his shirt until she didn't know how it stayed together. "You're just a little uptight, like this isn't in your comfort zone."

Well, it didn't take a genius to know that. She wasn't a violent, physical person. And she hadn't spent so much time with a man since Chris. It was just easier not to think about the husband and family she'd never have if she didn't stay in close proximity with men.

Except, ever since she'd met Tristan, she'd let him tote her around and hold her close without considering it for longer than a blink of her eye.

She'd needed his comfort the night before.

But today? Today she felt vulnerable for a completely different reason. Even if she couldn't quite put her finger on what it was.

He brushed his hair off his forehead. The skin at the corner of his eyes crinkled with a smile. "You'll do great. We'll take it easy today. Rome wasn't built in a day and all that."

His definition of taking it easy and hers were probably very different, but she agreed anyway. "All right."

"First, you have to recognize that you're probably not going to beat this guy on sheer strength."

"Says who?"

He picked up her arm at her wrist, and when he let go, it flopped to her side like limp spaghetti.

"All right. So I won't try to overpower him. Got it." She couldn't help the smirk that worked its way onto her mouth. "What's next?"

"Next, you do everything that you can to get away. Your goal isn't to win. It's to run."

"Got it. Next?"

Now his smirk matched hers. "Not so fast, speedy. Let's practice."

"You want me to run?" She hated running. Always had. It was about as fun as rubbing jalapeño pepper juice in her eye. Maybe not even that fun. She'd nearly failed high school P.E. because she couldn't finish the mile run. A mile walk? Sure. A run? Not unless someone was chasing her.

But someone was now.

He shook his head and chuckled. "No running yet. Let's start with the first things first." He took a few steps back from her. "If you think someone is following you or someone is about to attack you from the front, the best thing to do is to get loud. Attract attention." His eyes turned dark, his brows hooding the blue storms below. "We already know this guy wants it to look like an accident. He doesn't want to draw any attention to himself. So if he's coming after you, get loud. Got it?"

"Got it."

A quirk of his grin caught her off guard. "Now let's hear it. I'm going to come after you, and I want you to practice yelling."

After two years in a country where she had been expected to be both silent and invisible around men, she balked at the command. "What am I supposed to say?"

"Whatever comes to mind." He circled his hands in a rowing motion, inviting her to come at him. "Come on."

She swallowed and took a step toward him. "Hey."

He bent over at the waist, his shoulders shaking with silent laughter.

"What's so funny?"

"You're not inviting me over for tea." He snickered. "I'm a threat to you. I want you out of the picture, and the only way to protect yourself is to draw enough attention that I'll be forced to back off."

He took a menacing step toward her, and she sucked in a quick breath before expelling it with all of her might. "Back off."

He jumped, his grin spreading, showing off his straight, white teeth. "Better. Now try again."

She squeezed her eyebrows together and wrinkled her nose, drawing as much venom as she could from the terror of a very real pipe bomb and hit-and-run. Her heart pounded, a throbbing beginning at the point right between her eyes. "I said, back off!"

"Everything okay over there, L.T.?"

She jerked toward the woman who had poked her head into the workout room from the front desk area. The woman's hands were balled into fists, her stance announcing that she was ready for anything.

L.T.'s smile came back even broader than before. "And just like that, you've drawn enough attention to get help and shown him that you're not going to be an easy target."

The pretty lady with mocha skin pointed directly at Staci. "You okay, honey?"

"Yes. Thank you. Just practicing."

"Holler if you need something." The woman disappeared back to her post at the front desk.

"Pretty good, Hayes." She rewarded his compliment with a smile. "Step one. Get loud. This could be enough to scare him off. I hope so. And if it's enough to distract him, or throw him off, then you start running."

"Do we have to practice running?"

He shook his head. "Not today. We'll stick to indoor training today."

Did that mean that running would be outdoors? This just kept getting better.

"So what if I can't get away? What if there's no one around to hear and nowhere to run?"

He stepped toward her, invading her space and making her look all the way up just to watch his face. Her heart hammered in her chest. Of course, this was just practice. There was no need for her body to suddenly feel as tight as a violin string.

She shook out her arms, taking a couple quick breaths through her mouth.

He looked down the slope of his nose and over the rounded tip. "If you have nowhere to go, then you have to make me think attacking you is a bad decision. Let me know you're not going to let me steamroll over you."

"Wouldn't pepper spray work? I bet that would make you back off."

He shook his head. "It would. But only if used right. If you were to get flustered or scared and dropped it, you've given me another weapon to use against you. And there are steep penalties in California if you use pepper spray in a situation that isn't explicitly for self-defense. Let's stick to using weapons that you have on hand."

She leaned in even closer and dropped her voice to a

whisper. "You're going to teach me how to use my hands as a weapon? That could come in handy."

"Not quite. But you can use them to push me away."

Rats. That meant putting her hands on him. Something that was at once terrifying and far too appealing. Or maybe it was the appeal of touching him again that terrified her. She'd enjoyed the time in his arms the night before more than she wanted to admit even to herself. Tucked away in his embrace, she'd been safe, secure from whoever was after her and whatever that man was willing to do.

In his arms, she'd let her mind roam to dreams that were far better left undreamed. Thoughts of a future with a man who held her like that weren't safe. They weren't realistic. They weren't helpful.

They made her feel like every other girl who could dare to dream of a family of her own. But she wasn't like every other girl.

"Go on. Push me."

It couldn't hurt, could it? She needed the practice, as he'd said. She might need to use this someday. In a situation where it wasn't Tristan's arresting eyes staring down at her.

And that moment could come sooner than she hoped.

It was now or never. Taking a fortifying breath, she pressed her hands against his chest but jerked back as soon as her fingers encountered the steely muscles below the surface, her palms on fire.

"It's all right. You can push me. I'm not going to fall over."

Right. That's why she'd pulled back. She was afraid she'd topple a SEAL with her spaghetti muscles.

It certainly wasn't because of the flames that licked up her arms at the close contact. Or the butterflies that took his presence as a call to flight.

Clearly.

He stepped back into her bubble, and she mirrored his movement, keeping at least a few feet between them. Breathing room.

But he chased her, looking anything but an attacker. "Push me harder. Get used to the feel of it."

Getting used to the feel of anything between them was probably a bad idea. A very bad idea.

Tristan held up his hands to demonstrate the movement, flat palms facing away from him. "Don't try to hit or injure me. You're just trying to get away, trying to put enough space between us that you can run."

When she put up her hands to take another try, they trembled.

He dropped his voice, despite the empty room, so that Cassandra at the front desk couldn't hear. "Are you scared?"

"No."

He didn't believe her. And not just because she was a bad liar. Her voice quivered and her chin shook, just enough for him to notice.

"It's okay. I'm not going to hurt you. I'm not really coming after you. Just think of me as a practice dummy."

Her lips quirked to the side, a wicked glint appearing in her eye.

He laughed. "I know. I just set myself up for an easy joke. But pretend I didn't, and just push me away."

She nodded, her eyes narrowing into slits as she focused her attention on the front of his shirt. Taking three deep breaths, she lunged toward him, pushing into his stomach. As he took a step back to accommodate her action, a grin split her lips.

And then one of her hands slipped off of the flat plane

of his belly, her fingers trailing around his waist. With nothing to brace against, she slammed into his chest. He caught his arms around her, holding her steady as his pulse kicked into the next gear.

She stared up at him, her eyes alight with more humor. "Sorry."

"No problem."

He should have let her go. He should have just released her. But his arms tightened for a split second, his embrace holding her motionless.

A man could get used to having Staci Hayes in his arms.

"Should I try it again?"

"Right. Yes." He dropped his arms so quickly that she stumbled backward and only stayed on her feet when he grabbed her shoulders to keep her steady. "Try again. But this time, aim for a higher, wider plane." He patted his chest with both hands, showing her the target. "Hit me here. You'll have better leverage and more room to connect."

She nodded, once again narrowing her eyes, and licked her lips. His gaze locked onto the tip of her tongue as it swept across her mouth, leaving her lips pink and glossy, and ripe for kissing.

Like a double attack, he felt like he'd gotten a kick to his gut at the same time she shoved against his chest, her hand covering his heart.

He dropped to the floor like a plebe attacked by a seasoned SEAL, his arms and legs spread against the blue mat, completely prone.

In an instant, Staci hovered over him, her hair swinging forward around her face. "Are you all right? Did I do something wrong?"

Yes. She'd wiggled her way into his life, when she should have just stayed in her own. He was fine before he'd ever met her. Sure, he'd be happy to run the rescue mission again. But the "after" part. The part where she'd shown up at his office, so cute and funny and, before long, so clearly in danger that it made him want to protect her. Keep her safe. Make her smile.

It had been ages since he'd thought about Phoebe, but suddenly spending his life with a woman had her on his mind. And that just brought back the guilt, and the resolve. Never again. Once was too often.

"I'm fine." His voice was a little more growl than it should have been. Time to lighten the mood. He pushed himself off the mat with one hand and held the other out for her to help him up. When she latched on to his hand, he yanked it just hard enough to topple her. As she tumbled toward the floor, he swung his arm out and caught her back inches before she hit the mat.

She shrieked, pushing against his shoulder. "Let me go." But her words were garbled by the humor in her voice, her attempts to free herself weakened by laughter.

"You had that coming, knocking me over like that." He kept his words teasing for fear that she'd hear the truth of them. She had bowled him over. Not with her hands or force, but with her sweet presence in his life.

Having her near made him mourn what he'd been missing.

Matt and Ashley had found it. And he was glad they were happy.

But that didn't mean he deserved it. He'd had his chance.

Staci landed a shove against his shoulder, the movement pushing up his T-shirt sleeve, before righting herself on the floor. "Hey," he said. "Are you still trying to fight me?"

"Depends. Are you still trying to attack me?" She was sharp and funny, and when her smile grew, so did his heart.

Green eyes danced with glee as she leaned into him.

Or maybe he was leaning toward her. It was hard to distinguish at the moment.

Their laughter died down until even her smile dimmed. It wasn't unhappy, just thoughtful. Contemplative. And then she chewed on her bottom lip, all mirth gone.

Of its own accord, his hand reached to brush her hair behind her ear. His fingers connected with feather-soft strands at her temple, and his thumb stroked her scar. As he paid precious attention to the remnant of her time in that jail, she looked away from his eyes, instead following his arm up to his shoulder.

Suddenly her entire body tensed, and she lunged for the edge of his T-shirt, clawing at the sleeve as she pushed it up.

"What's wrong? What's—"

She jabbed at the edge of his tattoo, rolling the shirt partially out of the way, until just the lower half of the image was visible.

Her eyes wide and filled with alarm, she whispered, "He had that tattooed on his arm, too."

Tristan froze for an instant, the hair on the back of his neck jumping to attention and his ears ringing.

After a long beat of silence, he managed to say, "Grab your stuff."

"What—why? We just got here." She looked around, her head whipping back and forth to follow his movements as he jumped to his feet. "I thought we were going to do more training."

"Not right now."

He didn't bother waiting for her to pick up her gear; instead with one hand he snatched both of their bags from the floor. He rested the other on the small of her back as soon as she stood, ushering her out the door and into the noontime sun. Opening the passenger door of his truck, he helped her in, then slammed it closed when she was settled.

It wasn't until he threw their bags in the backseat of the crew cab and yanked his door closed behind himself that he took a real breath. It was loud and uneven and foreign to his own ears.

"L.T., tell me what's going on." Her voice shook like her hands had before. He'd never been so severe around her before. Well, not since the mission.

He leaned his right shoulder toward her, rolling up the sleeve of his shirt to expose the entire piece of art. "This? You're sure that this was his tattoo."

She nodded, but then shook her head. As she pulled down the edge of his shirt, she covered more than half the badge he'd gotten at twenty-three with others in his SEAL class after earning the designation.

Ten minutes before, he probably would have only been able to focus on her cool fingers against his skin, but now he held his breath in anticipation. What she said next could change everything.

"I only saw about that much. Just the bottom of it. This curved line and some of the pitchfork. But what I saw was just the same as yours." She shifted her gaze from his shoulder up to his eyes. Hers were big and round and filled with something he couldn't quite put his finger on. "Why? What is it?"

His throat hurt just to say the words. "That's an image of the trident pin given out only to United States Navy SEALs."

NINE

Tristan growled low in his throat, emotions coursing through his veins faster than he could process them. Confusion. Disbelief. Suspicion.

Anger.

If her face was any indication, Staci was dealing with the same onslaught. Her lips thinned and eyes narrowed until he couldn't see any of the dancing green behind her black lashes.

"What do you mean?"

"I mean, anyone who gets one of these better have graduated BUDs and been pinned a SEAL."

She was beginning to understand. He could see it in the tightening line of her lips and the tension in her jaw. "Everyone?" She wanted him to say that he was kidding or that some men just got the tattoo because it looked cool.

He wanted to be able to tell her that. But he couldn't.

"There was a kid in my SEAL class who was so confident that he wouldn't ring out that he'd gotten the trident tattooed across his back even before indoc."

She shook her head, clearly not following his story. "Indoc?"

"Indoctrination. That's the first three weeks of SEAL

training. It's where the first real cuts are made. It's weeks of unending torture—"

"Weeks of torture?" She was incredulous, but he lifted a shoulder and tipped his head.

"Wading into the ocean and then rolling on the beach— fully dressed and in the freezing cold. They called it 'getting wet and sandy.' But it was more like 'getting wet and trying to remember why I ever thought I'd want to be a SEAL.' And then realizing I had six more months of that.

"Anyway, this cocky kid—a state champion swimmer or something—walked onto the bus, looking like he was guaranteed a spot on the teams. But the only thing guaranteed in BUDs is that you'll have to work harder and be tougher than you ever thought you could.

"The kid rang out on his second day. He didn't like the salt water much. And he didn't like being harassed for that tattoo. I heard later that some guys didn't like him wearing that tattoo without earning it, and they told him so hard that he had to get a couple new teeth."

She shook her head, her eyes growing wide. "They beat him up for having a tattoo."

Tristan hated to sound so harsh in front of a woman who had seen plenty of pain, but he nodded. "Don't get me wrong, being a SEAL is hard work, but it's also an earned privilege. It's a brotherhood of the elite. Men have to earn that tattoo."

She swallowed, the sound thick and strained, filling the cab of his truck. "Then the man I saw…"

"Is or was a SEAL."

"Isn't there any possibility that he could have been like that kid? Maybe he got it but didn't make it through? Or maybe he got it to honor a brother or something?"

She was clawing for anything that might make sense of what she'd seen. He wished he could pull her into his

For Your Reading Pleasure...

Get 2 FREE BOOKS filled with riveting inspirational suspense featuring Christian characters facing challenges to their faith... and their lives!

Your 2 FREE BOOKS have a combined cover price of $11.98 or more in the U.S. and $13.50 or more in Canada.

 Peel off sticker and place by your completed Poll on the right page and you'll automatically receive 2 FREE BOOKS and 2 FREE GIFTS with no obligation to purchase anything!

arms like he had the night before to comfort her through her turmoil, but the bucket seats weren't exactly conducive to that. Besides, he had to think clearly. Having her close didn't bode well for the precision and speed of his mental processes.

"Maybe," he finally conceded.

"But not likely." She didn't even form it in a question.

"No. Not likely. The guy who left you the bomb is an expert demo man. Zig said he'd never seen that fail-safe line in action before, and Zig has seen nearly everything. And, like any SEAL, he has a full knowledge of the San Diego harbor and Coronado."

But she already knew that. She'd been the one to bring him the map, after all.

"We're not dealing with a wannabe or an admirer," he continued. "This guy is a pro, and pros don't usually run around getting ink they haven't earned."

"Will the tattoo at least help us narrow down our list of suspects?"

Only to every SEAL in history.

He bit back the quick remark. It wasn't entirely true. The trident hadn't been established until 1970, and the SEALs from the early years probably didn't have the dark hair that Staci had glimpsed in the jail.

He nodded slowly. "Sure. Now we know we don't have to bother with a guy who's not connected with the teams."

"And on the teams? How many guys would have that tattoo? A few?"

He shook his head. "Most."

She fell back into her seat, once again pulling her legs up and wrapping her arms around them. It was her safety position. He'd found her like that the night before on his couch, in her bathtub and even in Lybania.

Lord, let me make sure she never has to curl up like that again.

He pulled on his seat belt and started the truck, torn between taking her to his home and heading out immediately to question every trident-tattooed sailor on Coronado until he identified the person planning an attack on his hometown.

One glance at Staci, and the battle was over, the decision made.

She needed rest and security.

And attacking sailors on the base was more likely to get him court marshaled than help him discover who was behind the pending assault.

But he would find the person responsible. He just had to get Staci the opportunity to see others. Maybe if she heard his voice, or saw his shape or his gait, she could recognize the man from her jail.

Then Tristan could make sure that he was brought to justice. Even if he was a sailor.

His stomach dropped.

Or—heaven forbid—an active SEAL.

Staci scribbled nonsense words on a pad of paper, leaning an elbow on Tristan's table and holding her chin up with her hand.

The second will be first.

The second will be first.

"The second will be first."

"Did you say something?" Ashley called from where she sat on the couch, reading a book about what to anticipate upon her baby's arrival. Her hand moved in slow, absent-minded circles over her stomach.

Staci's heart squeezed, more with affection for her new

friend than with jealousy. When she offered a smile, it was genuine, and Ashley responded in kind.

"No. Just mumbling to myself."

They had been forced to spend more time together than Staci had first counted on, but after the near hit-and-run and the revelation of the conspirator's likely connection to the navy, Tristan had been adamant that they stay together and not leave the house without an escort.

After three days in the same house, she'd decided that if she had to be cooped up with a pregnant woman, Ashley Waterstone was her best option. She cooked like a pro, laughed easily and seemed sincerely concerned for Staci's happiness. Perhaps most important, she didn't ask too many questions. She seemed to know that whatever had brought Staci to Tristan's house kept her there.

They hadn't seen much of Tristan in the twenty-four hours since he'd dropped Staci off after her first self-defense lesson. He came home late and left early, but called at least three or four times while he was on the base.

When the phone rang, she knew somewhere deep in her stomach that it was Tristan. Or maybe it was deep in her heart, where the thudding picked up speed.

Ashley answered the phone. "Hello?…Oh, sure. Hang on." She held the receiver out to Staci, not even bothering to try to get up to take it to her. "He wants to talk to you."

"Me?" This was the first time he'd asked to talk with her, and she held the phone like it might bite her. "Hi?"

"Hey, Hayes. Everything going okay there?"

She stepped into the kitchen and lowered her voice. "All quiet on the home front, as they say."

"Good. No strange calls or lurking solicitors?"

"Nope."

"Good." He'd already said that. But she didn't remind him. Somehow talking with him on the phone was a flash-

back to high school. Her ten-year reunion was just over a
year away, but on the phone with him, she was seventeen
again, wondering what he was thinking and if he'd called
just to hear her voice.

Which was beyond ridiculous.

She was twenty-seven, not seventeen. Men didn't call
just because. They certainly didn't call women like her.

"I have an idea."

See? This was more than a check-in call.

"The navy is commissioning a new aircraft carrier next
week, and there's a ball on Saturday night in honor of it. I
have to go. Would you like to go with me?"

Suddenly she was a junior in high school again, her
mouth going dry.

But this was better than being asked to the prom. More
like Cinderella's night out.

Only there would be no prince coming after her at the
end of it. Princes—like any other men—wanted women
who were whole.

As if on cue, he quickly added, "I thought this would
give you a chance to meet a lot of men on the base—you
know, so you can listen to their voices. See if you recognize any of them. It might give us a lead on who's behind
the map and bomb. It's a long shot, but it's the only way I
can think to let you rub shoulders with nearly every officer on the base without drawing extra attention."

"Right." Of course. He was thinking about the mission.
Like she should have been. "That's a good idea. But what
about being recognized? Don't you think they'll wonder
why you're bringing me? You're not really supposed to be
seen out with me, are you?"

The pause ran long, like he hadn't thought that through.
"The news shows and papers aren't running pictures of

you anymore. They haven't been for about a week now, and the picture of you that they have is…"

"Not my best." She filled in the words for him because he was too nice to verbalize just how terrible the picture they had of her was. Some news group had taken a shot of her walking off the plane, her first time on American soil since the raid. But the wind had whipped her hair around her head and she hadn't been able to smooth it down, her arm still in a sling from the bullet she'd taken. She'd also been wearing the only thing the hospital on the base in Germany had—blue scrubs that added at least twenty pounds.

And it seemed to be the only picture the media wanted to use.

"Yes. I think in the dim lights of a party, wearing something that actually fits, with your hair and makeup all done up, no one will recognize you. Except maybe the man who's looking for you. But he wouldn't strike in a crowded situation like that—not when he still wants to make your death look like an accident."

"I'm in."

"Are you sure? I mean, if he's there, you could end up face-to-face with the man responsible for the pipe bomb and running you off the road and trying to run you over outside the shelter." His voice dipped with concern. If he was second-guessing his decision to invite her, she wasn't going to let him off the hook. This was her chance to point out the man who was not only trying to kill her but also putting thousands of innocent lives in danger with his bomb.

"I can do this. I want to."

"Good." His smile carried through the connection. "So, I'm off tomorrow," he said. "Up for another trip to the gym?"

Her butterflies took off again, and she clutched the phone harder than could ever be necessary. This was a call about a serious issue, but her stomach wouldn't listen to reason, so she tried to lighten the mood. "We're not practicing running, are we?"

He laughed. "Not a bad idea, but I was thinking something more along the lines of hand-to-hand."

Just the memory of their contact during their first session set her face aflame, her cheeks burning so bright that even from the living room Ashley gave her a strange look. Staci jerked her gaze away, staring out the window.

She took a deep breath. "Are you going to teach me how to take a man down with just my pinkie?"

He laughed, rich and throaty, like it had been a while since he'd used those muscles. Maybe since their last session. "Not quite. But at least how to hit him where it hurts the most."

She laughed then, too. "All right. First thing in the morning?"

"Yes."

He hung up without pomp, and she walked toward Ashley to place the house phone on the end table within her easy reach.

Without looking up from her book, Ashley asked, "What was that all about?"

"Nothing. He just wanted to see if I was up for—" She caught herself just before admitting to the self-defense training. That would just open the door to a world of questions she didn't have answers for. "Um...he wanted to know if I'd go to a party with him. For the commissioning of an aircraft carrier."

Dropping her book into her lap, Ashley clapped her hands. "We have to get you a dress. And shoes. And we'll get your hair and nails done."

"No. No. We don't have to do any of that. It's just a party."

Ashley's eyes and smile both grew wide with excitement, flashing white teeth as she spoke. "Oh, no, it's not. The navy doesn't just throw a party. They throw balls. Full-dress uniforms and beautiful gowns."

Running her fingers down the side of her face, Staci backed up until she fell into Tristan's overstuffed recliner. "Maybe this was a bad idea," she said through pinched lips.

"No, it's not."

But it was. It was a terrible idea. What was he thinking inviting her to a formal event?

She didn't fit in at galas like that. She was jeans and comfortable skirts, not floor-length gowns and updos. Her time in prison had left scars that didn't belong in a ballroom.

So had her surgery six years before. And those were just the visible scars.

Anyway, she and Tristan weren't supposed to know each other outside of her rescue. He'd told her that more than once that first day she'd come to his office. What would people think when they saw them together? This could get him into serious trouble, even if he assured her no one would recognize her. What would he do when someone asked for an introduction? This was all a bad idea. Maybe she should tell Tristan she couldn't go. That would solve the problem.

Avoiding the ball is also a convenient excuse to get out of spending time alone with him because you're afraid you might like it too much.

Ashley's smile slowly faded, and she looked at the book in her hands. "Can I ask you a question?"

Staci paused at the hesitation in Ashley's words. "All right."

"Please don't get me wrong, I'm thrilled that Tristan is taking you, but…" Her eyebrows bunched together. "You know what? Never mind."

A band around her lungs squeezed, and Staci leaned forward. "What?"

Shaking her head, Ashley's face became a mask of uncertainty and warring emotions. Finally, in a small voice, she asked, "Why isn't he taking Robin?"

Ashley asked the question as if Staci should know the girl, and her stomach twisted painfully. "I'm not sure. Who is she?"

"Oh." Ashley was definitely surprised that Staci didn't know about Robin.

So, who was she? Probably someone who would fit in at a navy ball. Someone without a red scar marring her face. Someone beautiful and elegant.

Someone whole.

Staci sighed as the mental image of a statuesque blonde in a figure-flattering gown on Tristan's arm flashed across the back of her eyelids.

That was the type of woman he'd want.

She didn't need to know Robin to know what type of woman he'd usually take to this kind of event.

Because whatever his type, it wasn't Staci.

He'd made that clear on the phone. This was part of uncovering the information on the map and keeping her safe from an American terrorist. He didn't want her. And she couldn't blame him.

The next morning Staci was ready for another training session just as she'd promised. But no matter how clear Tristan's instructions on the blue mat, she couldn't focus on anything but the image she'd conjured of his Robin. Who was she? What was she like? How long had they been together? Or not together?

"Hold a key between your fingers like this." He held up a fist, one jagged key protruding from between his middle and ring fingers, the rest of the key chain clasped in his palm. "See? Now try to hit me. Dig it in deep."

She nodded, taking the keys from him and doing like he'd shown. Except when she swung at him, her hand opened, and the keys clattered to the mat. They bounced twice, and she could do nothing but stare at them as he stooped to pick them up.

As he knelt on one knee with one forearm propped on the other leg, he gazed up at her.

She gasped, coughing on the sudden intake and concurrent lurch of her pulse.

If he only knew.

There, with mussed brown hair, wide blue eyes filled with compassion and an easy grin, he looked like he might be proposing. Except for the absent ring, everything about his stance called to her childhood fantasies of romantic proposals.

Even the unusual location fulfilled her dreams of a memorable tale to tell friends and family.

If she were another woman—any other woman—maybe he would have been.

Instead, he frowned up at her. "You okay? You seem distracted."

"Yes, well…" She couldn't very well admit that she kept picturing another woman in his arms, and it made her heart ache and her muscles limp. That when he held her, it made her feel like a real woman, if just for a few minutes, which made it all the harder when reality sunk back in.

His gaze dropped to where his hand wrapped around

the keys. "Want to tell me what's going on? You didn't say two words to me last night."

"I was tired."

"You went to bed at twenty-one thirty. Still tired?"

No. Yes. He didn't need to know that she'd stayed awake for hours, huddled under her covers, trying to force the picture of him with an imaginary woman from her mind every time she squeezed her eyes closed. That she'd finally given up and stared through the darkness at a ceiling she couldn't see because it was easier than wondering if he was in love with someone else.

She could only blink like an owl in response to his question.

Of course she was tired.

But that wasn't why she was dropping keys and throwing halfhearted punches.

"I'm sorry that you're under so much pressure. I know you probably don't want to go to the ball, but I can't think of any other way for you to interact with so many men on the base."

There. He'd just given her the out she'd hoped for. "But won't you get in trouble for being seen with me? We're not supposed to spend time together. You said so yourself."

He ruffled his hair with a flat hand, never taking his gaze from her face. "We'll fly under the radar as best we can. And I've talked to my superiors. They understand enough of the situation that we'll be in the clear." The corner of his mouth rose in a lopsided grin. "Besides, you won't look much like your picture in the papers, and we'll just keep from using your last name as much as possible."

Her shoulders fell, her breath escaping through tight lips.

"If you could pinpoint the voice of the man you heard in Lybania, wouldn't it be worth it?"

He thought she was upset about going to the ball. He thought that's why she kept dropping things, bumping into walls and refusing to answer his questions.

If only he could understand that the minute she spoke, she knew Robin's name would fly out of her mouth.

It was eating her up inside not knowing who Robin was and what she meant to him. Not knowing if she had grown far too fond of a taken man. Even her concern about the gala stemmed from her uncertainty about Robin.

She rubbed her eyes with her fingers, blinking her contacts back into place until the contours of his hair came into focus. She managed two quick breaths, trying to formulate some sort of response. Some kind of explanation.

She wanted to go to the ball with him. She just didn't want to go when there should be someone else on his arm.

She wanted to hear the voices of the other men on the base, searching out a familiar lilt or recognizable phrase.

She wanted to find the man she'd heard inside her jail cell and make sure justice was done. And then she wanted to go back to her old life, where she didn't spend every day in close quarters with a man who insisted on making her long for a different destiny.

But her words fell short.

And vanished altogether when he put his hand on her waist.

It was heavy, his fingers splayed over the small of her back, his thumb rubbing a slow circle on her side, a gentle prodding to open up to him. Beneath long, pale lashes, his eyes implored her for something more than broken glances and trembling hands.

She took a fortifying breath. "I want to go, but…" Her words were more air than sound, so she cleared her throat before continuing, torn between wishing that he'd pull his hand away and that he'd keep it right where it was forever.

Chewing on her lip, she closed her eyes and just let out the truth as fast as she could. "Don't you think Robin might be upset if you take me?"

He jerked his hand away, and a chill swept down her side in the absence of his embrace. "Robin?"

She risked peeking at him through one eye. His eyebrows reached toward his hairline; his mouth hung open.

"How'd you hear about—" He cut himself short. "Ashley." With eyes reflecting an internal storm, he shook his head.

"Please don't be mad at her. When I told her about the ball, she just asked why you weren't taking Robin." Suddenly the words wouldn't stop flowing, and she didn't want them to. "And she didn't tell me who Robin was, but I just figured that there was someone special in your life, and I wouldn't ever want to get in the way of that. And this is important—but maybe there's another way. I just don't want to be in the way. And I don't want Robin to be mad. And maybe she'd feel better if she could meet me. Or knew that there was nothing going on." She flapped her hand between them, feeling ridiculous with Tristan still on bended knee. Pushing the terrible nerves in her stomach away, she opened her mouth to plunge forward.

Maybe if she just kept talking, she'd pass out and hit her head hard enough to forget that she'd ever blabbered on like this, as he kept a perfectly straight face.

"This isn't Ashley's fault. She's just concerned about you. And I'm a guest in your house, and…"

Her words died on her lips as the corner of his mouth slowly rose, his eyes gleaming.

Ever so slowly, he stood, his hand brushing her arm and no more than a breath between them. When he was all the way upright, he bent his head, looking straight down into her eyes, his smile now full-blown.

"I guess I never got around to telling Ashley."

"What?" The word was a croak. But it was all she could handle as her skin buzzed with his nearness.

"Robin hasn't been in the picture for more than a year."

TEN

Tristan stumbled back as Staci pushed flat palms against his chest, the force of her impact catching him off guard.

"You jerk," she said.

"Good hit." He laughed as he caught her wrists in his hands and tugged her closer.

"You let me just keep going on and on." Her chin bent low. Long hair hanging over her shoulders, she shook her head. "Why didn't you stop me?"

His smile dimmed as he tucked her hair behind her ear. But he didn't really have an answer for her. At least not one that made any sense. He couldn't just tell her how cute she'd been, her eyes so filled with concern.

"You should have stopped me. I sounded like an idiot." She sighed, still not looking up from the piece of mat between her tennis shoes. "Maybe I am one. A useless idiot."

His fingers drifted up her arms, until he cupped her elbows. The space between them vanished. Battling the tension around his heart, he skimmed his fingers back down her arms. "You're not an idiot. And you're most certainly not useless. I'm a jerk. You're right. I should have stopped you, and I'm sorry. I wasn't expecting you to ask about Robin. I didn't think you knew who she was."

"I don't."

He held her at arm's length then, ducking down until he could see her face. Glistening pink lips had all but disappeared as she chewed on them, her jaw in constant motion as she ran her fingers down the side of her face. She refused to look at him, and the band pulled tighter around his chest.

Taking a shallow breath, he shot a glance around the room. When he was certain they were alone, he said, "I didn't tell Ashley because I didn't want her to know."

Big green eyes, filled with curiosity, fluttered up at him. "What didn't you want her to know?"

"That Robin and I stopped seeing each other."

As though he'd spoken the invitation, she slipped her hand into his, holding it as though she could squeeze the hurt from his past. "I'm sorry."

He took a quick step back, suddenly unsure of what to do with the hand she'd captured. He'd had no problem holding her close to comfort her before. But this reversal of roles where she consoled him didn't sit quite right.

Of course, that didn't mean he was eager to let go of her hand, either.

He just had to keep himself from getting used to the feeling of having her around. It wouldn't last forever. It couldn't.

"Why didn't you want Ashley to know?" Her words were as gentle as the breath that tickled his arm.

The short version. He could just keep it simple. She didn't have to know the whole story, the part that still felt like a knife to his chest every time he thought of it. He didn't want her pity or need her sympathy.

And he most certainly didn't want to relive his most terrible memory—what happened with Phoebe that made his relationship with Robin doomed from the start. No, he wouldn't bring that up.

Especially not in front of this woman, who carried her own tortured past.

"After Ashley and Matt got married, my sister started worrying about me. Worried that I'd end up old and alone."

"You're not old. Not yet, anyway."

He laughed. "Thanks for that."

Her head tilted back, her eyes filled with concern. "Why would she be worried that you'd end up alone?"

Oh, the million-dollar question. The one guaranteed to give him heartburn. He'd rather face down another building full of tangos than answer her question. Her words held no contempt or unkindness. She hadn't meant to dredge up old memories and the bitter past.

But he couldn't tell her.

"Was there someone else before Robin?"

He didn't have to say it. He didn't have to answer her question. He did anyway. "Yes."

Staci's thumb on the back of his hand rubbed in a soothing circle, and he let his shoulders relax, the tightness in his chest releasing. Maybe he could tell her a little. Just enough to satiate her curiosity.

"Her name was Phoebe."

"Tell me about her."

It had been more than four years. He'd dated Robin since then, been promoted, and even learned to be happy for Matt and Ashley. But the memory still crashed through him, stealing his breath and leaving his muscles limp. How could he speak the words?

It was better to avoid them altogether, right?

Better to dodge the truth, cover the emotional scars and keep it together.

Even better to walk away before he began longing for something that he didn't have a right to want. Something that couldn't be his.

Something that was more and more attractive the longer he held on to Staci.

But he couldn't be both a SEAL and a spouse. He couldn't be abroad saving the world and save his love, too.

Phoebe had proven that.

So then, why was having Staci this close so sweet?

Oh, Lord. His breath caught on the two-word prayer, his chest a battleground of agony as he pulled Staci into his arms and thought of Phoebe.

He didn't want to think about her. He didn't want to talk about her. And he couldn't give up her memory.

Staci leaned into him. "I mean, you don't have to say anything if you don't want to."

Good. He didn't want to. But his mouth didn't get the message, and suddenly he was talking about her. "We met when I was just out of SEAL school. She was incredible. Funny and smart and intent on being a veterinarian. She loved animals, always bringing strays back to her apartment. I think I fell in love with her the first time she made me pull over on an old two-lane highway to check on a wounded dog. We took it to a pet hospital, and she held on to my hand so tight that I couldn't feel my fingers anymore. And then she cried when the vet said the mutt was going to be fine thanks to her.

"I'd never met anyone like her. So full of life and joy. Always checking in on her elderly neighbors and volunteering at the humane society. She said it kept her busy while I was deployed."

"Were you gone a lot?"

"I did two six-month tours while we were dating. She never complained, so I knew she was the one. I proposed the day after I got back from my second tour."

Staci wrapped her arms around his waist. "She sounds

perfect." There was a note of something pained in her voice, but he couldn't quite put his finger on it.

"She almost was."

Silence surrounded them. Staci was waiting for the rest of the story, but he didn't know if he could tell it. Didn't know if he could survive another chest wound. Rehashing the past didn't do him any good. He'd never talked with Ashley about it, barely said two words to Matt right after the funeral. There wasn't much to say.

"What happened?"

He'd never said the words aloud. Four years and everyone who should know did. He'd never had to speak them. A fist around his heart made him doubt if he even could. But he wanted Staci to know. For some reason it was important that she understand his past and why they could have no future. He squeezed his eyes closed and took a deep breath. "I was on a short mission, and she was killed in a carjacking gone wrong about a month before we were supposed to get married."

He shook his head and dropped his arms. He couldn't hold Staci so close and grieve for Phoebe, too. It was just too much. Stepping back, forcing Staci to release her grip as well, he stared into her face. Pity and tears shone in her emerald eyes, but she didn't look away.

"I am so sorry." She blinked and rubbed a knuckle under each of her eyes. "I didn't know."

Jabbing one hand through his hair, the other firmly planted on his hip, he did the last thing he normally would. He looked away. It was too hard to meet her gaze. "I was gone, and I couldn't protect her. I lost my chance for a future and a family in a split second. And I was thirteen thousand miles away."

He covered his head with his hand, bending his neck until his chin met his chest. His words were still tinged with bitterness, the pain still so acute. Yet somehow he felt the tiniest bit lighter inside.

Had he missed out by not talking about this with someone before?

When she finally spoke, her voice shook, like she was the one with all the regrets. "I'm glad you told me." She slipped her hand back into his and said, "Let's go home."

Staci wrapped an escaped curl at her temple around her finger, then slowly pulled her hand away as it bounced back into place.

"Your hair is so pretty up like this."

She glanced up to meet Ashley's eyes in her reflection, and they shared a smile as Ashley pushed one more pin into place. Only an abundance of hairspray and bobby pins could keep her dark hair swept up into the French twist, a few loose locks framing her face. "Thank you for helping me get ready for tonight."

Her lips parted as her smile reached all the way to her eyes. "There's nowhere else I'd rather be."

Staci shifted her gaze back to the vanity mirror in Ashley's room. Despite the perfect makeup that Ashley had meticulously applied, she turned just enough to see her scar, its presence a reminder of everything she'd faced, and everything that was yet to be revealed.

"If only…" There were too many to say them all. If only there was no scar. If only she'd never been in that prison. If only she were just a woman dressing up for an evening out with a man who really cared for her. If only Tristan could be that man.

If only she could be the woman he deserved.

She clamped her shimmering lips together and closed her eyes against the rush of wishes.

She didn't have to be bitter or angry about the things

that would never be. She didn't have to long for them. It didn't do her any good.

There was no wishing herself whole.

Four days before at their training session, Tristan had said he'd hoped for a family. When he was ready again to look for love, he'd look for someone who could give him what he wanted.

It wouldn't be her.

Ashley's voice in her ear stopped her fingers from brushing across her cheek. "Try not to touch your face. Especially right there."

"All right. I'll try." But she couldn't make any promises as the lump in her stomach swelled with every passing moment.

In less than an hour she'd be on the base at Coronado. She'd be among the navy men, listening, searching for a familiar voice. And if she heard it?

What then?

The rock that had been a petty annoyance in her stomach suddenly burst. What then, indeed? Would she motion to Tristan, and he'd just know? And would he confront the man then and there?

And what if the conspirator recognized her first? What if he knew her and tried to keep her silent?

Sweat burst onto her forehead, and Ashley was there in an instant, dabbing an oil-free pad against the makeup. "I'm not sure what happened. It looked great a moment ago. Are you too warm?"

"Just nervous, I guess." She rubbed her damp palms against a tissue instead of on the green silk dress that skimmed her legs.

"Don't worry. Tristan will take care of you tonight. You'll have a good time."

She was sure of the first, but the second remained to be

seen. Despite her dry mouth, she managed to swallow the fear that bubbled up just as Tristan knocked on the door.

"You about ready in there?"

Ashley let him in while Staci picked up her purse and a sparkling black wrap that wouldn't even begin to keep her warm against the evening chill blowing in off the ocean. But somehow her black hooded sweatshirt didn't quite match the flowing silk that reached just to the top of her strappy black heels.

With clutch and scarf in hand, she looked up and straight into Tristan's unblinking eyes. Everywhere her skin danced with goose bumps, as if his gaze was tangible. Immediately, her hand shot up to cover her scar, but she stopped just in time at Ashley's quick shake of the head.

"You look—" His voice broke, and he cleared his throat. "You look…really nice, Staci."

"Thank you." She tried to keep the disappointment from her tone. Three hours of dress shopping with Ashley. Two and half hours on her hair and makeup. And she still only looked "nice."

Right. Nice.

She shouldn't have hoped for more, and she began to chastise herself for it. But as her gaze swept over him, she lost track of every thought except how good Tristan looked in his uniform. His black dress shoes shone in the overhead light beneath crisp and perfectly creased black slacks. His matching black jacket boasted a row of small medals over his heart above the parallel rows of three shimmering gold buttons. A black bowtie at his throat topped off the immaculate presentation. Even his usually tousled hair was a little bit straighter, a little more polished.

The smirking smile was just the same as during their training sessions, though.

"You got a haircut."

"There's going to be a senator and a handful of admirals there tonight. Thought I should look my best."

Mission accomplished.

He held out his hand, and she slipped hers into it. Despite all the contact they'd had at the gym, every time he'd held her and the time he'd thrown her over his shoulder during her rescue, this felt like the most intimate contact they'd ever shared.

"You kids have fun," Ashley laughed as she held the front door open for them.

"You will call if you need anything?" Staci turned back at the last minute.

"Of course. But I won't need anything. I'm absolutely fine." She rubbed her hand over her belly. "Still two weeks to go and not a contraction in sight. You both have a good time." Then she dropped her voice to a conspiratorial whisper. "You look amazing, Staci."

He led her to the driveway where his truck sat. "Are we taking that?"

His eyes narrowed. "What else would we take?"

She looked down at her skirt then back up at him. "I might need a hand."

Understanding lit his eyes in a flash. He walked her to the passenger side and pulled the door open. Pinching a piece of silk between her thumb and finger and lifting her skirt out of the way, she moved to put her foot onto the running board.

But he beat her to it, sliding his hands around her waist and lifting her into the seat as if he'd done it every time she'd ridden in this truck.

He disappeared, slamming her door behind him.

Just perfect. Their evening was off to a great start. First he hadn't thought she looked pretty. Only nice. Which was fine. She didn't need his appreciation or affirmation.

Really.

But now he couldn't get away from her fast enough.

Between the expectations for the evening, the possibility of facing a man who was part of a conspiracy trying to kill her and Tristan's stiff silence, she was ready to run back inside, put on her sweats and spend the evening with Ashley.

Who'd have ever guessed that she'd prefer the company of a pregnant woman—and all the reminders that brought—to a night of formal finery with the most handsome man she'd ever seen?

When he was in place behind the wheel, he turned the key in the ignition, the engine rumbling to life. Without a word he backed out of the driveway, navigating toward the base. He refused to look in her direction, so she stayed facing straight ahead, but her eyes persisted in searching him out.

When she thought the silence would never end, he said, "It's probably going to be crowded at the officer's club, so I want you to stick by me. All right? We don't know if he's going to be there, but I don't want to risk losing track of you if he is."

She pinched her eyes closed, the extra coats of mascara sticking as her top and bottom lashes pressed together. Focusing on the discomfort kept her mind off the tightness in her chest—the one that told her his words hurt. She'd wanted to hear something else.

But she didn't have a right to.

He'd promised her nothing beyond his protection.

So why did his sudden coolness make her lungs burn?

"Got it, Hayes?"

"Yes, Lieutenant Sawyer."

As an afterthought, he added, "And remember, we shouldn't use your last name too liberally. People may not recognize your face, but on this base, in this company, they'll almost certainly recognize your name. We don't need to draw undo attention."

Just Staci. No last name. She could remember that easily enough.

But if he didn't want to garner attention, he shouldn't have put on that uniform.

ELEVEN

Tristan gripped the steering wheel until his knuckles turned white. Anything to keep his attention on the road in front of them. Anything to keep his eyes off of the vision in shimmering green sitting by his side.

Anything to remember that he had no right to harbor the feelings building in his chest, the desire bubbling just below the surface of his skin.

And acting on it?

He couldn't come up with a worse idea.

She deserved so much better than a man who couldn't protect his own. And he couldn't leave a woman behind again. He wouldn't.

He slammed the door a little harder than necessary, gulping lungfuls of the brisk twilight air and praying for a clear head. *God, let me keep her safe tonight.*

If they couldn't move forward with intel on the case that night, they had no other leads to follow, except the map, which was proving to be more enigma than tool.

The second will be first.

Still their only clue. Still no help.

The tattoo was a slow lead, at best. Tracking down the whereabouts of all the possible SEALs was no easy task. Commander Harding, who oversaw the teams at Coronado, had promised to look into which teams they could cross off their list of possible suspects, but that was bound to take weeks. And it didn't account for retired SEALs, who were every bit of a possible threat. Tristan had requested a list of demo experts for the past twenty years from the teams— men who could have built the bomb at Staci's house—but the process of getting that information could take years.

Their plan tonight needed to work for so many reasons. Not the least of which was his own sanity. If they couldn't make headway, Staci would go on staying with him indefinitely, wiggling her way into his heart and life until he couldn't bear the thought of her leaving.

But for her sake, he had to let her go.

As soon as possible.

He straightened the line of his uniform jacket, flattened his bowtie and smoothed a hand over his fresh haircut. Marching around the front of the truck, he opened her door and held out his hand as she slipped from the seat, spinning toward him as her toes touched the parking lot pavement.

Of its own accord, his arm encircled her waist, but he jerked it back just before making contact, instead turning his attention to the flimsy wrap she drew over her otherwise bare shoulders. Two tiny straps on either side of her neck crossed in the back, caressing her skin and holding her dress in place.

"Lieutenant Sawyer." He jerked around at the sound of his name, coming face-to-face with a commander who had been in a recent meeting with the CO, Captain Crawford, but whose name he could not remember.

"Sir. Good to see you."

"And who do you have with you tonight?" The other man's eyes roamed over Staci, whose blush was clear even in the dimming evening light. She pulled the black gauzy thing tighter around her shoulders, her fingers fisting into the fabric below her throat.

This was not the time to play coy or to keep his hands to himself, so he slid an arm around her back, holding her firmly to his side and sending a clear message to the commander and anyone else watching that she was with him. "This is Staci."

The man nodded slowly and held out his hand to her, offering a slight bow, his medals glinting in the parking lot lights. "Commander Carter Garrison, United States Navy JAG Corps."

She glanced at Tristan for a split second before turning her smile toward Garrison. "It's very nice to meet you."

"Oh, no. The pleasure is all mine. I hope you'll give me the honor of a dance later this evening."

Smarmy and unctuous. As Garrison strolled away, Tristan smacked his tongue several times, trying to clear the bad taste that the other officer left.

"He seems nice."

He shot a hard glare at Staci, only to find her on the verge of a giggle, hand covering her pink lips and shoulders shaking. Well, at least she had enough sense not to fall for Garrison's over-the-top charm.

Some of the tension drained from his shoulders, and he held out a hand to show her the way. It was an important night, but it didn't have to be torture. In fact, as they ate prime rib and the port's finest seafood, the slow throbbing behind his eyes began to fade.

Staci was a natural, resting an elbow on the table and cupping her chin in her hand as she leaned toward the woman seated to her right, who was telling a mind-numbing story about a whale-watching tour that had been an abject failure. But based on Staci's body language, it was the most thrilling thing she'd ever heard.

Tristan would have given up the view of the beach from his backyard just to have her look at him the same way. Or to laugh for him like she did when the woman's husband suggested they make parties like this a regular part of navy life.

The wife elbowed her husband. "Well, if these were regular events, how would we celebrate the big to-dos, like commissioning new aircraft carriers?"

Their little threesome laughed until the officer picked up his glass of wine in a salute. "Then to the *USS Rockefeller,* an excellent reason to put on dress blues and dance with the prettiest girl in the room." He squeezed his wife as the band, which looked like it could have come straight from a World War II–era USO party, struck up a tune. Tristan immediately tapped Staci's shoulder and held out a hand. "Care to dance?"

Her gaze narrowed in on his fingers, then moved back to his face. Finally she nodded, slipping her hand into his and letting him pull her to her feet as she excused herself from the conversation she'd been having with the middle-aged couple.

He pulled her into his arms as they slipped around the dance floor, drawing close enough to other dancers to hear just the lilt of their voices, but never the words.

Telling himself that this was important, that this opportunity to mingle with other guests was the reason she was here, he gave himself permission to enjoy the feel of her in his arms, the way she fit into his embrace.

But only just.

"You're a pretty good dancer," she said after several songs.

"Thanks." He'd stop there. No need to tell her that his high school football coach had made the entire team take dance lessons to improve their footwork.

Suddenly she tensed, every muscle under her hands shaking.

"What's wrong? Do you see him?"

"No. It's her." She ducked into his chest, hiding behind his shoulder, but never quite brushing her cheek against his jacket. Glancing up at him with big, round eyes, she chewed on her lip. "It's my public affairs officer. She'll recognize me for sure."

Funny. He hadn't thought about her for a second. He'd just been so happy that Staci had agreed to join him to-night that he hadn't considered any of the people that she'd already come into regular contact with.

Pulling her even closer to him, he spun them until he could watch the PAO dancing with a man in a black tux. She shook her shoulder-length black hair and smiled up into the face of her partner, not at all interested in them.

"I think we're safe. But keep your eyes open for her."

"Uh-huh." Her response was more a sigh than actual words as she finally rested her head against his right shoul-der.

This was exactly what he didn't need. Where had the space between them gone?

Right. He'd pulled her against him and held her for all he was worth the moment he thought there was danger. But now the only danger was the reappearance of emo-tions he'd hoped long buried.

Time to put that space back between them. Anything to make him think about the real reason they were there. "Have you heard anyone familiar?"

She shook her head, brown curls at her temples bounc-ing. "No. But I've only spoken to a few men, and then only very briefly. I think I need to really interact with them."

He hoped his frown told her what he honestly thought

of that, even though he gave her a more gentle verbal cue. "I don't think so."

"Then this is a wasted opportunity. How much trouble can I get into if I'm on the dance floor and you're watching me closely?"

"Could go either way. You have a knack for finding trouble."

Her smile made him forget why he'd been trying to keep space between them, trying to stay unattached, when she was so sweet, so funny. But a tap on his shoulder derailed that train of thought. He spun to find himself face-to-face with Captain Crawford.

"Sir?"

He couldn't be much into his fifties, but years at sea had left the XO with a weathered face, which broke into crinkles as he smiled. "Mind if I cut in?"

Yes. Of course he minded. He didn't want another man touching her. As sure as the tides, he didn't want to let her go. But when she gave him a gentle smile and stepped into Crawford's waiting arms, Tristan didn't have much of a choice.

He backpedaled off the floor, bumping into a fellow lieutenant and her partner because he couldn't be bothered to take his eyes off the swirling green dress.

When he finally found his seat, he sipped his water, never letting his eyes wander far. Even as she changed partners, blushing and batting her eyes at each man, he kept track of her. With each new man came a pang in his stomach and an ache in his chest, and he grumbled into his glass as the songs changed. His leg wouldn't stop bouncing, his stomach twisting tighter and tighter with every passing minute.

The waiter with a white napkin folded over his arm refilled Tristan's water glass three times. Still Staci danced, flirting and giggling with every partner.

Why didn't she flirt with him? He could make her laugh. He *did* make her laugh. Sometimes.

After almost an hour, he could take no more torture. Standing and thumping his glass back on the table so hard that he rattled a few pieces of silver, he walked toward the sea of dancers, his gaze trained on the curve of Staci's throat as she threw her head back with a laugh.

But Captain Crawford stepped into his path, forcing him to stop. "Good to see you here, Lieutenant Sawyer."

"You, too, sir."

Crawford thumped him on the back, a grin in his eyes. "You brought a very pretty date tonight."

Where was this conversation going? He didn't know, but he didn't have any choice but to respond with the truth. "Yes, sir."

"She's very familiar." Dark brown brows swooped low over his pale blue eyes, and he elbowed Tristan in the side as Tristan battled a rush of cold dread. Crawford knew who she was. "Does she hang out at the pool hall?"

Maybe Crawford didn't recognize her after all.

Clearing his throat, Tristan grasped for something to say, something that would excuse him from this increasingly awkward conversation. "I don't think so. She's a friend of my sister's." That wasn't a lie. And it didn't imply anything amiss.

"Uh-huh." The older man—still fit and trim in his uniform—rubbed his hands together. "A bit young for you, eh?"

"We're just friends, sir." It wasn't a lie, not really. He wasn't interested in just being her friend—but friendship was all he had to offer. "Well, I better check in with her. Good evening."

He slipped away, headed in the direction where he'd just seen Staci and her most recent partner, a kid fresh out of college. But she wasn't there.

He spun slowly, surveying every corner and shadow for her flashing eyes and matching dress.

Nothing.

His gut clenched and his palms turned sweaty.

With a strained breath, he strode into the gaggle of spinning couples, eyeing every profile, even as the growing tension in his chest told him that he wasn't going to find her. Most of the faces were familiar. Crawford and his wife. Several SEAL officers from other teams. The PAO who Staci had been deftly avoiding all evening.

But none of them were the face he wanted.

Maybe she'd stepped away to check her makeup or catch her breath. After all, she'd been dancing all evening. He forced himself to take even strides down the short hall toward the restrooms. The narrow corridor was empty except for one blonde woman in a striking red dress stepping out of the ladies' room.

Throwing away caution, he gave her his best smile. "Excuse me, ma'am. I seem to have lost my date." He managed a chuckle, despite the fear that wound around his throat and threatened to choke him.

Her laughter carried all the way down the hallway and into the party. "You certainly wouldn't be the first man to say that." She nodded toward the wooden door with the gold placard announcing Ladies. "I'll just check in here. What's her name?"

"Staci."

The woman disappeared, and he held his breath, staring at the reflection in his shoes. *Lord, please let her be in there.*

"I'm sorry." He jerked back up to meet the blonde's

laughing gaze. "There's no Staci in there, but there are two girls commiserating about their terrible dates. Just be glad yours isn't among them." She waved as she passed by him, returning to the party.

He plunged a hand into his pocket, pulling out his phone and hitting the button to connect with Staci's. She should have it in that sequined black purse she'd held like a lifeline the entire ride from the house. Of course, if he hadn't been such a jerk, maybe she wouldn't have had to cling to something like that.

The phone rang.

He'd just been too stunned seeing her like that. Every bit the vision he'd never imagined when she'd been wrapped in a burka the first time they met.

It rang again.

She was all soft skin and beautiful lines and bashful smile. At that moment his interest in her had had absolutely nothing to do with protecting her and everything to do with finishing that almost kiss they'd started at the gym a few days before.

One more ring.

She made him wish things with Phoebe had been different. Or at least that he'd walked away from that pain less certain of his own failures as a fiancé and future husband.

By the fourth ring, his stomach was in knots. And when her voice mail clicked on, he slammed his phone against his open palm, already running for the side exit and the parking lot.

Like a winter wave from the Pacific, the truth stole his breath.

Staci had vanished right in front of him.

TWELVE

"I'd really rather go back inside." Staci tried to jerk her arm out of the commander's grasp, but his fingers pinched her elbow until pain shot up to her shoulder.

"Don't be ridiculous. It's hot and stuffy inside, and look at that moon." He stumbled on his words, the *S* sounds catching on a lisp. Not heavy or overly pronounced, and probably more noticeable since he'd been drinking. The smell of liquor on his breath fell over her like a second wrap, clinging to her skin with sticky fingers.

He tried to drag her through the open front door of the club, and she raised her voice again. "I don't want to go. Back off!"

The music from the band drowned out her cry, and since he was nearly twice her size, he had no trouble hauling her from the building and toward his car.

She spun as much as she could in his grasp, looking for anyone nearby, hoping that Tristan might have followed her. That's what he had said. She just had to get loud enough to attract help. "Leave me alone!"

The commander sidled up to her, his free hand grabbing her chin and holding it still as he breathed over her. Swallowing a gag, she pulled back until she was flush against a car. "You don't know what you want. You've danced with every sailor in there tonight, but I've seen you look-ing for me, waiting for me to make you mine. I don't want to wait any longer."

"Help!" She spat the word over his shoulder.

And with a crash, he was gone, swung into the side of the opposite car. She jumped out of the way, grabbing her throbbing elbow as she stared into Tristan's twisted fea-tures. But he wasn't looking at her. His eyes were slits, focused on the man in front of him.

Tristan breathed hard through his nose, towering over Commander Garrison, a forearm pressed against the other man's throat.

The commander cowered, his head shaking as he tried to push Tristan away. "Don't. I wasn't doing anything." He could offer no more than a croak around Tristan's arm.

With a shaking hand, she touched Tristan's shoulder, and he spun around. "It's not him."

Confusion replaced the anger in Tristan's eyes and he shook his head. "But he tried to get you away."

"Yes, but he's not *the* one."

Tristan must have let off the pressure against Garrison, who took a ragged breath.

"Are you sure?"

"He has a lisp. The other guy didn't."

He nodded slowly. "Did he hurt you?"

Her elbow would have a bruise, but the rest of her body was unscathed. Her sanity, on the other hand, was not so lucky. "No." Mostly she just wanted Garrison to leave so that Tristan could hold her. So that she didn't have to think about all the things that could have happened if he hadn't shown up.

A fraction of the tension in Tristan's face ebbed away, and he turned back to the quivering man. "You need to go sober up. And on Monday I'm going to report you for conduct unbecoming an officer in the United States Navy."

"But I outrank you."

Tristan jerked his chin toward Garrison, who jumped back. "Do I look like I care?"

The instant Tristan removed his arm, the commander bolted for his car. "I'm sorry. I've got to call this in." Tristan held up a finger as he spoke into the phone. She could barely make out his words through the ringing in her ears. Something about an intoxicated driver on base.

When he hung up and put the phone into his pocket, she was ready to fall into his arms. But he didn't hold them out to her or invite her into his embrace at all. He just stared at her, his face a mask devoid of emotion. He'd had no trouble showing Garrison his anger and iron-fisted control, but for her he had nothing.

Her chin quivered. Maybe from the crash of adrenaline following the scary ordeal. Possibly from the rush of relief at Tristan's impeccable timing.

Both were unlikely.

It was almost certainly from Tristan's rejection.

She dipped her head and raised a hand next to her ear. Before she could get there, Tristan caught her wrist in his loose grip, gently returning it to her side as she looked up with wide eyes. His gaze didn't meet hers, instead it followed his hand, which trailed down her scar, this thumb caressing the jagged line.

"I'm sorry that I lost track of you. It won't happen again."

"It's okay. You found me in time."

When he finally met her gaze, the emotions he'd kept from his face swam in his eyes, soft as his touch and just as warm. "You're sure you're okay?"

"I think so." Except that the circles of his thumb on her

cheek were making her stomach dance in the same gentle motion. Couldn't he just hold her and erase the memories of Garrison's touch? She blinked at him, hoping he would understand her thoughts.

Whether he did or just followed his own desire, she'd never know. What she did know was that his arm wrapping around her waist was exactly what she needed. Safe and secure in his embrace, she stepped to his chest until there was nothing between them but her hands on his starched jacket and her trembling breaths.

"It's going to be all right." He pulled several loose pins out of her hair, sending tendrils falling down the back of her neck. "I'll take you home."

She wasn't ready to go yet. She didn't want to leave this haven.

Apparently he didn't, either.

Letting out a slow sigh, his shoulders relaxed, but his grip tightened. The hand on her back stilled and his breathing stopped.

She sought out his gaze, again hoping that this might be the moment she'd been dreaming about. Wishing that he'd make good on the promise of his actions at the gym. That she'd have at least one chance to know the feeling of his lips on hers.

His head dipped low, his breath warm against her lips.

She hadn't kissed anyone since Chris. She hadn't felt like she had anything to offer a man since him.

But now she saw in Tristan the tenderness that Chris had never shown. The kindness and concern that left her boneless and weak against him. That left her craving his touch.

When he finally completed the motion, pressing his lips to hers, her eyes fluttered open for a brief moment, just long enough to catch a glimpse of the serenity etched into every line of his face.

She let herself go, falling down and down but always in his arms. He pulled back for a breath before kissing her again, this time with more vigor but no less wonder. She leaned against him for fear of collapsing without his support, a sigh escaping as she slipped her fingers over his jacket and into impossibly soft hair at the nape of his neck.

He smelled of spicy aftershave and tasted like chocolate cake, suddenly two of her favorite things.

Time lost all meaning until a door slammed and boisterous voices filled the night air.

She stepped away, a chill immediately sweeping down her arms.

Tristan ran a finger down the curve of her jaw, the smile she'd hoped for conspicuously absent. "I should get you home."

As Tristan pulled his truck into his driveway and turned off the headlights, he sat in the dark for several long moments of silence. Only the shallow breathing from Staci in the seat beside him filled the cab. Squeezing his hands together, he stared out the windshield, hoping for any words that would help him say what had to be said.

The drive back from the base had been silent, and he still had no words to change that. He could ask how she was feeling, but that just opened up a world of possible emotions that he couldn't respond to. He could just get out of the truck and act like nothing had happened, but she deserved better than that.

He could kiss her again.

He wanted to. But that wasn't fair to her, especially when he should only be focused on keeping her safe.

He should never have kissed her, shouldn't have let himself get so carried away.

It had been sweet torture holding her close and knowing that he couldn't repeat their kiss or the roiling emotions swelling in his chest.

It was best to stick to the mission and their reason for going to the ball in the first place.

"So, you're sure that Garrison isn't the man that you heard?"

"Yes. He has a lisp and a very faint Southern accent." She must have turned toward him, as her voice shifted directions, but he couldn't see her in the darkness. "It wasn't him."

"Any luck with anyone else?"

"It was so loud in there, and there was only one who, for a second, I thought could be him, but it turned out to be a white-haired commander, who said he'll be retiring soon."

"Not him?"

"Definitely not. The man with the tattoo had strong muscles, firm skin and dark hair. Not a kid, but definitely not a man approaching retirement."

He dipped his chin to his chest, staring at the outline of his folded hands, inky blackness consuming them. "So I guess tonight was a bust. We didn't learn anything new."

"We eliminated at least a few possible suspects."

"Leaving only a couple hundred more." His words were more bitter than he'd intended, and he bit back the next words that came to mind, waiting until he could put a more positive spin on the situation. But he didn't have to when she jumped in.

"I did have another thought, though."

"What's that?"

"Well, stay with me for a second. Maybe it's a stretch,

but I think I have an idea where the explosion might happen."

He sat up straighter, staring toward her eyes. "Where?"

"The map shows the harbor, right? So what if this is all to do with a ship? What would make a bigger statement than blowing up a naval vessel?"

"But there are dozens of ships of all shapes and size, in and out of the harbor every month."

"Right. So that got me thinking about what was written on the map. 'The second shall be first.'"

Where was she going with this? Her voice picked up volume and speed as her excitement grew, but he couldn't follow the direction of her thoughts. "How does that tie into a ship?"

"It's something that the captain at our table said. He toasted Nelson Rockefeller. I thought the new carrier was named for John D. Rockefeller, but he assured me that it's the *USS Nelson Rockefeller*."

"As in, Gerald Ford's vice president?"

"As in the second in command." She paused to let it sink in. "I asked if there were a lot of other ships named for vice presidents, and the captain said it wasn't very common."

His stomach swooped, and he grabbed for her hands before he could second-guess the action. He rolled her words over and over, looking at them from every side. "If the tangos want to make a statement—and something planned like this is guaranteed to—they'll have the attention of news coverage, senators, the governor and probably every Rockefeller heir on the West Coast."

"You don't think it's ridiculous?"

"I can't believe I didn't think of it. It's logical and an incredible statement against the country. And if your theory is right, the person responsible will have full access to the base. We'll need to watch the base closely and especially the carrier." He squeezed her hands. "Smart."

The weight on his shoulders hadn't exactly lifted. It had just been replaced by a new set of worries. But at least he could contact his CO and let him know what they suspected. And he could call his friend in the FBI counterterrorism unit for some extra backup. This wasn't going away, but at least they weren't floundering without direction.

After he walked her inside, locking the door behind them, they stood at the foot of the stairs for a long moment. The kitchen light, which Ashley had left on, shone brilliantly compared to the darkness of his driveway.

He shoved his hands into his pockets to keep from reaching for her.

She looked up the stairs, then back into his eyes. "Thank you for tonight."

Was that gratitude for letting her get dragged away by a man too intoxicated to know how to treat a lady? Or for the two dozen dance partners she'd had to endure without any hard leads? Or for the kiss?

Please let it be for the kiss.

"Good night, Tristan."

His name sounded like honey on her lips. It would be far too easy to get used to that.

After church the next morning, Staci spent the afternoon on the couch, watching her football team clobber their rivals. In her pale-blue-and-yellow jersey, she cheered them on—as loud as she could get and not disturb Ashley, who had insisted she just needed a short nap three hours before.

From his seat in his recliner, Tristan would look up from his newspaper and smile in her direction every now and then. After halftime, he gave up reading the paper and joined her on the couch, cheering for the opposite team.

"What are you doing? Don't you want San Diego to win?"

"I'm not from San Diego. I moved here for the job. I'm rooting for Kansas City all the way."

His crooked grin and the glimmer in his eye made her question if he was telling the truth, or just being contrary to tease her. His phone rang before she could prod him, and he grabbed it from the end table, glancing at her over his shoulder as he disappeared into the kitchen.

In a low timbre, he responded to the call, but she could hear only the reverberation of his words and not what he was actually saying. She tried to watch the game, but her mind kept wandering toward the next room.

When he returned, his face was like stone, his hands clenched into fists.

"What's wrong?"

He sat down next to her, but instead of facing the television, he angled his knees toward her. "I've been called in on a training mission tomorrow night."

She licked her lips and stared at the ceiling, playing out the scenarios that this could cause. "How long will you be gone?"

"Just twenty-four hours. But I don't have a choice. I have to go."

She nodded. "I know. I understand. We'll be fine." She wasn't sure if she said it for his benefit or hers, but he leaned toward her, his elbows on his thighs. "We'll be fine," she repeated. "The commissioning isn't until Wednesday, right?"

"Right. But I don't feel good about leaving you here alone with Ashley."

"Don't worry. I'll take care of her." Who'd have ever thought she'd be volunteering to care for a pregnant friend?

"I'm not just worried about her. I'm worried about you."

Chewing on her lip, she looked away, reminding herself that he was concerned for her safety. His words didn't go deeper than that. "I'll be fine. We'll stay close to the house." And as an afterthought she added, "Maybe you could send Will or someone to check on us."

"I can't. The rest of the team will be with me on the training op."

"Right."

She was about to be completely unprotected for the first time since she'd tracked Tristan down to his office on the base. Since he'd taken her under his wing. Since he'd started shoring up the broken pieces of her heart.

"I know how to make enough noise to scare him off if he shows up." Her smile quivered, her attempt at humor falling flat.

He shook his head, rubbing his chin with two fingers. "Don't try to take him on, Staci."

"I won't. I promise."

"And you'll stay close to the house? You won't go anywhere that he could catch you alone?" His eyes narrowed, leaving only slits of blue that flashed with something like concern—only infinitely more intense.

"I won't."

"And you'll yell if there's any—" Interrupting himself, he jumped up and ran to the kitchen.

Abandoning the football game, she chased after him until she caught him at the kitchen's junk drawer, which was surprisingly organized with cubbies and dividers. After just a moment, he produced a silver whistle and held it out to her. "Keep this on you. Put it around your neck. You're not going for subtle. You're going for safe. If you think for a second that there's someone following you or getting close, blow on this thing until help comes."

She took the noisemaker, and he kept his eyes on her

until she bent her head to loop the chain over her neck. "Thank you."

"You're welcome." His gaze was physically heavy, pressing her shoulders down and sending a chill along her arms. She hugged herself, wishing for the courage to either walk away or stare back just as hard. But after the kiss they'd shared the night before, she could do nothing but try to keep her stomach from dancing a jig.

Finally he whispered, "I don't want to leave you alone, but I don't have a choice."

"I get it. We'll be fine."

He reached for her, cupping both of her shoulders with his lean fingers and adding physical pressure to the force of his gaze. "Listen to me very carefully." Waiting until she nodded in response, he took a shallow breath. "The man behind this knows what he's doing. That pipe bomb wasn't a joke and neither was that van that tried to run you over. If our guess is right that he plans to sabotage the *Rockefeller*, then he has too much at stake—too many eyes watching—to let you ruin this for him."

She tamped down the fear that bubbled through her chest and up her throat. This wasn't new information, but the intensity in his tone left her trembling.

"He will come after you. Don't let him find you alone and unprepared."

THIRTEEN

Long after Tristan had left for his training op the next day, Staci sat up with a very uncomfortable Ashley.

"Can you turn the air a little higher? It's so hot in here."

Staci pulled her scarf a little tighter under her chin, wishing that she had a winter hat to match. Her fingers almost numb, she punched the thermostat button until the air conditioning unit kicked on again, the temperature dropping across the first floor in minutes.

From her prone position in the recliner, Ashley sighed. "Thank you."

"Do you want some more water to drink?"

"Yes. Please." She held up an insulated jug, the ice rattling as Staci filled it up to the top. "I'm sorry you have to put up with me."

"I don't mind a bit." Strangely it was true. Every minute watching Ashley carry a baby—like Staci never could—should have been painful. But it wasn't. A little catch in her throat or a pang in her chest were the only reminders that this was what she'd dreamed of but could never have. The rest of the time, she felt nothing but empathy and joy for her friend—and wonder at the life that was being created. "Are you comfortable? Do you need anything else?"

"Cotton candy."

"What?"

Ashley's eyes grew wide, her smile spreading quickly as she rubbed her hand around and around the T-shirt covering her stomach. "Doesn't that sound fantastic? Just good old-fashioned carnival cotton candy."

"Not really."

"I have to have some."

Oh, dear. Tristan still hadn't told Ashley that they couldn't leave the house, that they weren't safe outside. And he hadn't given Staci any suggestions on how to deal with pregnant cravings. It was easy enough to stay indoors when that's where Ashley wanted to be. But what about when she wanted to leave?

She needed an alternative. Something to satisfy Ashley's craving without having to leave the house. "What about ice cream? That's sweet and we have a freezer full."

Ashley wrinkled her nose. "No. Too milky."

"All right. I think Tristan left a few of those coconut cookies you like so much." She jogged into the kitchen, yanking open the pantry door. Her stomach dropped at the sight of the empty shelf where the package had been. "Never mind."

"It's okay. I want cotton candy. Pink cotton candy that will stick to my fingers and melt on my tongue." Her voice rose as the recliner squeaked to her rocking motion. "And I know just where to get some. Let's go to Belmont Park!"

Staci leaned her head against a cupboard door. *Lord, give me the words to talk her out of this. I can't protect her out there. I can't even protect myself.*

"It'll be dark soon. Let's go to Belmont another time." The small carnival right off of Mission Beach was guaranteed to have the cotton candy Ashley craved. And hundreds of places for someone to hide, just waiting for a chance to pounce. On the other hand, it would also have hundreds of other people milling about the midway. If someone attacked her, she could yell for help, or use her whistle, and someone would be sure to hear.

But she'd promised Tristan they wouldn't leave. She couldn't take Ashley. Yet if she didn't, there would be questions that she couldn't begin to answer.

As Staci stepped back into the living room, Ashley held out her hands with a sheepish grin. "I can't get up."

As Ashley rocked in the chair, Staci pulled her hands until she was on her feet. "Oh!" She jumped, pressing a hand to the side of her stomach. "He's not very happy that we're on the move. See? Feel him kicking."

Staci shook her head as fast and hard as she could. "No. No." The words little more than a mouthed refusal.

But Ashley had Staci's hand pressed against the rhythmic kicks of the little life inside before she could pull away. And then she didn't want to withdraw, as the clear outline of a foot pressed against her palm over and over. The little blessing at once swelling and breaking her heart.

"He's so ready to make his appearance."

"Are you ready?" As though she even needed to ask. Ashley was born to be a mom, cool and collected and sure to make her child's home a happy one.

"I will be, as soon as Matt gets home. He's supposed to be back on Wednesday morning."

"Just in time for the commissioning event."

"That's right." Ashley glowed. "But I'm not ready to do this without him, so he better not run late."

Staci smiled, letting her hand fall away from the spot where the little guy's movements had slowed to a less intense cadence. "I'm sure he'll be here." She had to turn away and clear her throat as her eyes glazed over with unshed tears.

What would it be like to love someone so deeply and

to be so certain of his love in return? To know that they'd get to share a life and a family?

She rubbed her knuckles over her eyes, plastering a quaking smile into place. There was no call to feel sorry for herself. She had a full life, and she would continue to find ways to keep herself busy and useful. And maybe—someday—she'd meet a man not interested in having his own family.

Tristan's face flashed across her mind's eye, and she clamped her lids shut, fighting the wish behind that image.

He wasn't going to be the one for her. No matter how well he kissed or how much she wanted a repeat of the night before. She'd take all the fear of being at Garrison's whim in exchange for Tristan's arms wrapped around her again.

But Tristan had been clear when he'd told her that he had wanted a family with Phoebe. He almost certainly still wanted the same thing.

Thinking about it wasn't going to help her be more content where she was. And it certainly wasn't going to help her stay alert for the dangers that lay ahead.

"Are you all right?" Ashley's voice dropped to a whisper.

"Yes. Sorry. Just something in my eye." Her cheeks hurt from smiling so hard, but she forced herself to look natural as she turned back toward her friend. "What do you say we find something for dinner?"

"Like cotton candy?"

"No. Not cotton candy."

"Don't trifle with a pregnant woman and her need for sweets. I won't give in." She put her hands on her hips, again with the mini linebacker stance. "Even if it means I have to go alone."

"Don't be ridiculous. I'm not letting you go anywhere

alone. But don't you think it'll be kind of cold after the sunset right off the water?"

Ashley grabbed the collar of her T-shirt, fanning her face and letting out sigh. "I'm counting on it."

All of her arguments for staying at the house were failing. But she couldn't let Ashley go alone. What if she went into labor? Or she fell down? Or was in a car accident? Tristan—and even Matt—were trusting her to keep Ashley safe until Matt's return.

"I don't want you to go alone."

"Good. Get the keys. Let's go. Right after I use the restroom." Ashley disappeared down the hallway.

Maybe Tristan would have an idea for stopping her. Grabbing her phone, Staci called his number, praying he'd be able to pick it up. With every ring, she glanced over her shoulder, checking for Ashley's return. When it went to voice mail, she whispered, "It's Staci. Ashley wants to go to Belmont Park for cotton candy, and she won't take no for an answer. I just don't know what else to do but go with her. I'll be careful, and we'll stay in well-lit, public areas. But...I just wanted you to know that I tried to talk her out of it. And I... Thanks for the whistle." She gripped it through her shirt and took a steadying breath. They'd be okay.

She tilted her head back and stared at the white ceiling, sending up a silent prayer for protection.

"Ready?"

As she'd ever be.

After the initial briefing on the night's op, Tristan packed his gear away into his trunk but stopped to check his cell phone before locking it inside. He rarely did that anymore. Hadn't since Phoebe, really. But maybe he'd received a return call from Victor Salano, his friend with the FBI.

Right. That's who he was hoping to hear from.

He had two messages, the first one started as the rest of his platoon filed past him, purposefully bumping into him. He shot Willie G. a scowl, and the kid grabbed his back and mimed walking with a hunch.

Tristan snorted. He wasn't a grandpa yet, just because he'd been around for a while. He had a few good years left with the teams, and he fully intended to stick around to keep Willie G. in line for a long time.

The message did turn out to be from his FBI contact. "Sawyer, this is Salano. It's good to hear from you. Listen, we intercepted some communications that line up with your suspicions about later this week. Can't talk about it over an unsecure line, but we need to touch base. Something is going to go down, and right now you're our man on the front lines. Call me as soon as you can."

His blood pounded through his veins, his heart picking up speed. Staci had been right. The map. The translation. The attempts on her life. All of it was about the *USS Nelson Rockefeller.* The ship named for a vice president was the tangos' first mark.

He checked his watch. Just three minutes until wheels-up. He didn't have time to call Salano back.

The phone switched to the second message, and suddenly Staci's urgent whisper rang in his ear. She sounded desperate, but he could do nothing from the base. Nothing from the air where he would be in a minute. He jabbed the button to return her call, squeezing his fist tighter with every ring. No answer.

"L.T., you coming?" He waved off Zig.

The chopper blades were already spinning as her outgoing message played.

He had exactly ninety seconds to tell her everything running through his mind, convey every shooting pain through his chest. But he wouldn't have been able to express that if he'd had ninety hours. In the end he took a deep breath and said between clenched teeth. "Staci, be careful. I need you to be there when I get back."

He hung up, throwing his phone into the locker and slamming it closed. The last one onto the chopper, he jumped in just as it lifted off the ground.

Staci's green eyes flashed across his mind as he stared out over the city lights. Somewhere out there was the woman he cared for. And a man intent on silencing her forever.

And he could do nothing about it.

Staci grinned as Ashley pinched the pink cotton candy from the stick and opened her mouth wide to push it in. It disappeared as her smile erupted, her eyes rolling back in delight. "This is just what I wanted." She had to raise her voice to be heard over the clacking of the white, wooden roller coaster and the screams of the children lifting their hands as the bottom fell away, sending them flying down the track.

Red and yellow lights from the carousel danced off Ashley's blond bob as she shook her hair out of her face against the breeze from the ocean, just steps away. She held out her stick, a silent offering of the sugary treat.

"No, thanks." Maybe it was the combination of the smell of hot dogs, popcorn and ocean that made her stomach churn. More likely it was the knowledge that she and Ashley were completely unprotected amid the crowd at Belmont Park.

"Let's walk for a bit." Ashley savored another fluffy bite, a low hum from her throat confessing her satisfaction. "Not far. Maybe just down to the end of the walk-way and back."

That was a good hundred yards or more, but they were already out. Ashley wouldn't give in to going home yet. So Staci nodded as they strolled through the crowd, weaving between families exiting rides, kids pointing and laughing at the fun they'd had. As they walked past the open wall of a bumper car ride, lights flashing and reflecting off the glittering cars, they paused. Little ones screamed with joy, steered themselves into collisions with other cars and screamed again. Moms lined the railing, the lights from their cameras adding to the vibrant night.

Ashley pulled off another piece of cotton candy, popping it into her mouth and licking her fingers in the same motion, but the smile that had accompanied every other bite didn't appear.

Staci watched her closely for several long seconds. "Is anything wrong? Are you feeling okay?"

"Fine. I was just thinking about Phoebe."

She sighed. What was she supposed to say?

"I guess my brother didn't tell you about her, either."

Staci squinted toward the kids on the ride, the words still elusive. So she spoke softly. "He's mentioned her."

Amazement filled Ashley's face as her cheeks went red and her eyebrows rose. "He has? He told you they were engaged?"

"Yes."

"And that she died?"

"Uh-huh."

Ashley let out a sad laugh, not bitter, just pained. "I think you're the first person he's ever talked with about her."

She'd gotten that feeling, too. When she'd stood with her arms around him, trying for all the world to comfort him like he had her. But she'd come up short. Again unable to give him what he wanted—even if he didn't know what it was he craved. Talk of Tristan and Phoebe left her stomach aching and her eyes burning.

She didn't want to ask questions or pry into his life, yet when else would she have a chance to hear the story from another perspective, to see how the loss had really affected him? The part of her that liked him more than any guy she'd ever known, the part that had been falling head over heels for him since he'd burst into her life, screamed for her to drop the topic, to keep her distance from any new knowledge of him that might make her fall for him even further. The part of her that longed to know him more didn't listen.

"What was he like back then? Was he going to stay a SEAL after they were married?"

"I think at some point he'd have retired. Not right away, but eventually. Probably when they were ready to have kids. But I think he thought of their engagement as the beginning of the end of his career on the teams."

Staci's heart squeezed, its beats coming erratically, as though she could feel his pain, know the loss that he'd had. It physically hurt to think about his story.

"Afterward, when he came home for the funeral, I thought he'd quit the teams right then and there. He still had a few years to go, but he was going crazy with pain." Ashley bit off another piece of her treat. "But I'm glad he didn't. He threw himself into his work, and found some sort of healing rescuing others."

Tears burned the back of her eyes, too many emotions rushing through her. Her heart broke for his pain. And at the same time, she knew in the depth of her soul that he'd never have rescued her from her jail cell if Phoebe had lived. The dichotomy of his sacrifice and her selfish thoughts warred within her chest, and she pointed to a cement bench partially hidden beneath branches from a green bush.

Ashley didn't need much prodding to keep talking. Maybe she just needed to tell someone, too. "He blames himself for not being here. He has it in his mind that if he'd just been stateside, he could have protected her, that maybe he could have saved her. As if he could have done anything to stop someone from carjacking her on her way home from work even if he'd been across town instead of out of the country."

It was ridiculous. And so very much like him to take responsibility when it wasn't his to shoulder. He'd done that with her, after all. He'd taken on her care and protection because she had nowhere else to go. He'd made it personal.

How much more so would it be when he really loved the woman he wanted to protect?

Ashley grabbed her hands. "I just thought you should know. I've seen how…close you're getting, and I love my brother very much. I'm just not sure if his broken heart has ever fully healed."

Staci looked away. She couldn't explain why she was even in their lives or how Tristan made her wish she didn't have her own broken pieces.

But Tristan was not beyond repair. He could learn to love again, forgive himself for being away and move on. She didn't have that opportunity. What was wrong with her would never heal.

People rushed past them, ignorant of the tumult of emotions washing over her. Their voices dancing and jumping, they motioned with their arms spread wide, their faces alight with the joy of the beautiful night and the twinkling lights on wires crossing above them.

All seemed to be alive with the night.

Except for one man. His nondescript gray sweatshirt pulled to his chin, he kept his back to them, facing a kiosk of toys and games. But somehow it felt like his eyes were on her, tangible despite the fifteen yards between them.

She squeezed Ashley's hand. She was being paranoid. He was just like any of the others enjoying the evening.

He'd move on in a moment.

Any second now.

Except then she'd lose track of him. Was it better to keep an eye on the man who gave her goose bumps or risk being surprised? What would Tristan say?

"I am so sorry to lay this all on you tonight." Ashley had obviously mistaken the sudden tension in her hands and arms for her emotional reaction to Tristan's story.

Staci swiped at the tears still pooled in her eyes. There would be time to talk about this more when she and Ashley were safe at home. Now she had to get them back to the car. But to get to the parking lot, they were going to have to walk past the man spending too much time staring at stuffed carnival toys.

When he pulled his baseball cap lower over his face, shivers ran down her back, setting her hair on its end. He glanced over his shoulder, round sunglasses covering most of his face. He was working too hard to keep his face hidden. Something was definitely not right.

She scanned the crowd for help. There had to be a security guard or police officer around, but she found none.

Tristan had told her to not be an easy target. Make noise and push back. Go for the shins with her heels and groin with her knees. If this guy wanted her, he was going to find a fight first. She grasped the silver whistle beneath her shirt with shaking hands.

"Staci? Staci, what are you looking at?" Ashley sounded like she'd called her name several times.

"Um..." *Oh, Lord, I'm not supposed to get her worked up. I'm not supposed to tell her what's going on. I'm not even supposed to be here!*

She silently prayed for help, but no thunderstorm provided an instantaneous exit strategy. No SEALs fast-roped in to protect them. No big burly men materialized as stand-in bodyguards.

And the man in the gray sweatshirt stayed right where he was, watching her in the reflection of the kiosk's mirror.

It was time for action. They had to move or be sitting ducks. And that meant that no matter what Tristan said, she had to tell Ashley the truth. She grabbed Ashley's arm, squeezing it just enough to convey the seriousness of what she was about to say. "Listen to me very carefully. There's been a man following me since I got back to the U.S."

Ashley's eyes flashed wide, then narrowed. "What does he want?"

Best to keep it simple and direct. No need to add more panic or raise Ashley's blood pressure any more than it probably already had been. "That doesn't matter right now. What matters is I think he's here. We have to go. And we have to go quickly. If you hold on to my arm, can you run?"

Ashley looked down at her stomach as though it were a foreign object, a brand-new addition to her body, and shook her head. "I don't think so." Her voice wobbled, but she paused and added in a stronger tone, "But I can move quickly."

Staci patted her hand, putting on her best reassuring smile. "We're going to be fine. We just need to walk with purpose and try to stay with a group. I don't think he'll try anything in public." She didn't add that the dimly lit parking lot would be another story altogether. They couldn't afford for him to follow them closely. And they couldn't lose track of him, either. Knowing his location was far better than the alternative.

Helping Ashley up, Staci waited for a chattering group of teenage girls to pass before following closely behind them, positioning herself between Ashley and the man in the gray sweatshirt. "Stay by me," she whispered. "And whatever you do, don't let go of my hand."

Ashley nodded, holding her head high, but her breaths were shallow, her free hand wrapped across her middle. The motion of her hips and belly looked as uncomfortable as it probably felt, but she marched forward.

As they passed the bumper cars and approached the arcade, Staci risked a glance over her shoulder.

Her pursuer was just yards behind them, nonchalantly weaving through the crowd, his unfamiliar face staring straight in her direction. She gasped, looking from side to side for someone to help. Nearing the carousel, the crowd began to thin. Almost to the parking lot. Then what?

Ashley's fingers bit into her arm, and Staci held on to her with both hands.

What had Tristan said? Get loud. Get in his face. Tell him she wasn't going to be his victim. It was now or never. At least here there was a crowd. And maybe help.

She slowed enough to speak directly into Ashley's ear. "He's still there. I'm going to try to scare him off. All right? Stay right here by this fence."

Ashley nodded, transferring her hold to the fence lined with unsuspecting parents watching their children turn circles on brightly colored horses.

Staci took a stabilizing breath and sent a prayer heavenward before spinning on her tennis shoe and marching toward the man in question, who had closed the gap between them to only two steps. "Back off!" Her voice barely rose above the din, only a few heads turning in her direction.

A twisted smile crossed his lips. "You've caused more than enough trouble for me."

Was that a lisp in his voice, or was she just trying to find something to tie him to Commander Garrison—anything to put a name to the still faceless man?

She tried to push against his chest, but he caught her wrist, wrenching it behind her. "Get off me! Let go!" She kicked at his shins but managed only to bump into a woman standing next to them as he tossed her around.

More heads were turning, but no one stepped forward.

With her free hand, she yanked on the whistle chain, getting it to her lips and managing one ear-splitting shriek before he ripped it from her mouth with a slap of the back of his hand. Despite the sting that seemed to follow her scar from her hairline almost to her jaw, she continued yelling, not at all sure that her voice could be distinguished from that of the roller-coaster riders.

And then another arm grabbed her attacker, small hands clawing at his arm. Ashley had come to her aid. What was she thinking? "Get back." Her cry again faded into the surrounding noise.

In the split second that Ashley turned her attention away from the man, he shoved her, and she fell to the cement walkway like a ragdoll. Her cry of pain couldn't be mistaken for the shouts of joy. Finally, the people around them began to react.

"Someone get that cop!"

"Help that lady!"

"Call an ambulance!"

Blinded by anger, Staci clawed at her attacker's hand until he yelped in pain, and she thrashed her leg around until it connected with his shin.

"Hey, what's going on here? SDPD."

Her attacker's hand dropped and he was gone, vanished

into the crowd and beyond before the fresh-faced bicycle cop reached them.

Staci fell to Ashley's side, grabbing the pale woman's hand. "Are you all right? I'm so sorry. I didn't mean for this to happen."

The officer rushed to them and squatted on Ashley's other side. "Ma'am, are you hurt? Do you need me to call an ambulance?"

Ashley's big blue eyes were filled with tears, giant drops streaking down the side of her face, as she met Staci's gaze. Cradling her baby bump with her free arm, she blinked. "I think something happened to the baby."

FOURTEEN

Staci clung to Ashley's purse and huddled into the corner of the ambulance as it wailed through traffic. From her tiny seat she could do nothing but hang on and try to keep her thudding heart from beating out of her chest as they rocked around the corners.

Ashley held out a hand toward her and mumbled something that was blocked by the oxygen mask over her mouth. One of the paramedics pulled it down for a second, and she said, "Call Matt."

"No cell phones in here, ma'am." The young woman in the blue uniform offered an apologetic glance before putting the oxygen back into place.

Ashley closed her eyes, and Staci reached for her hand, holding it with a firm pressure that she hoped reminded Ashley that she wasn't alone. "I did. Remember? When we were waiting for the ambulance, I left him a message, and Tristan, too." Weak fingers squeezed back and then released.

Ashley's prone form on the gurney suddenly went blurry. Staci blinked quickly to ease the pressure of the tears that insisted on flowing. Swiping at her eyes with the back of her hand, she offered a gentle smile. "It's going to be okay." *God, please let Ashley—and the baby—be okay.*

What-if scenarios danced through her mind, and she longed to have the day back. She should have just told Ashley the truth before they went to the park, explained why they couldn't leave the house. Because then if her blood pressure had gone up, it still might have triggered labor, but Ashley never would have been pushed to the ground. She never would have been hurt trying to come to Staci's defense.

Her stomach clenched around the sure knowledge that this was her fault. She was responsible, and she'd failed to keep them safe.

"Both heartbeats are slowing down." The male paramedic pulled his stethoscope from Ashley's stomach before calling to the driver. "Make sure the hospital has the on-call OB ready. She's bleeding."

If anything bad happened to the baby...

She couldn't even finish the thought, so painful were the knives in her chest. In just a short time, she'd come to love Ashley like a sister and care for the baby like one of her own nieces.

How could she live with herself if something was really wrong? If there was permanent injury to either mother or child?

Her prayers didn't have words, only silent cries to her Heavenly Father for healing and safety for the two lives on the gurney.

If only Tristan would call her back. He'd know how to contact Matt. He'd know what to do.

The ambulance pulled to a stop at the hospital with a surprisingly smooth motion, and the back doors flung open to the bright lights of the hospital bay.

"Sit tight." No one addressed her directly, but she knew the order was for her, so she curled into a ball as they pulled the rolling bed out of the vehicle and popped the legs into place. The female paramedic jumped off the back bumper, holding a bag of clear liquid above her shoulder, the other end connecting to an IV in the back of Ashley's hand.

Staci scrambled after them, chasing them to the double glass doors until a nurse in green scrubs held up her hand. "Are you a relative?"

Staci shook her head.

"Sorry, honey. Family only." The nurse pointed toward another door. "You can wait in there."

"But..."

There was no time. The gurney disappeared down the hall around a corner, and she stumbled into the waiting area filled with plastic chairs. The vanishing adrenaline left her weak, and she sank into the uncomfortably curved chair, letting her head fall into her hand.

The minute that her other wrist touched her knee, she jerked back, pain shooting to the bone. She curled her wrist under her chin, cradling her arm against her body and waiting. Just waiting.

After minutes that felt like seconds when she confronted her attacker, every moment in the E.R. waiting room felt like an hour, each tick of the clock agonizingly slow.

She wiped a hand across her face, her fingers coming away sticky with blood. Pressing a finger to the corner of her mouth, she gasped at the pain in the simple motion. The bitter, metallic taste of blood on her tongue made her cringe, and she stood up in search of a restroom.

The fluorescent light over the mirror above the single sink in the ladies' room wouldn't have been flattering on the best of days, but after a hand-to-hand battle with a powerfully built man standing at least a head taller than her, she cringed at her reflection.

A dark bruise was already forming on her cheek where he had hit her when she blew the whistle, and a trickle of red emerged from the same corner of her mouth. A brown mark marred her forehead, and her eyes were swollen and red. Likely a gift from all the tears she'd shed at Ashley's side.

Strangely enough, the only normal part of her face was the red scar in front of her ear. It didn't stand out quite so much amidst the other marks and bruises.

She jerked the lever to release more of the paper towel roll and ripped it off before slipping it into warm running water. With ginger movements, she dabbed at the corner of her mouth, washing away the blood until only the red cut was left. Then she scrubbed at her forehead and splashed water over her face, drops running down her neck and into the ripped and stained collar of her shirt.

After five minutes she felt more normal than she'd expected, save for the aches and pains in her arm and the ringing in her right ear, which was almost certainly from the smack she'd taken to the face.

She'd survived her first real brawl.

But would Ashley and the baby be so lucky?

She hurried back into the waiting room and locked on to the front desk. A triage nurse glanced up from her paperwork, holding out a clipboard. "You don't have to put up with that kind of treatment, sweetheart." She put down the clipboard for a moment and held out a brochure for the Pacific Coast House.

Staci shook her head. "No. I was attacked. By a stranger. Not... I'm not being..."

The woman's mocha-colored skin wrinkled around her dark chocolate eyes as she squinted. "Are you sure?"

"Yes, ma'am. I was with my friend, who was brought in in the ambulance. Is she okay? Can I talk with her?"

"What's her name?"

"Ashley Waterstone. She's pregnant."

The woman's fingers clicked on her computer keyboard, her brows pulling low over her eyes as they went back and forth across the screen. "I'm sorry, hon. I can't give you any information about her condition."

"But I was just with her." She pointed over her shoulder to the ambulance bay. "We came in together. She fell, and she said there was something wrong with her baby. Please."

The nurse's eyes were kind, but her tone never wavered. "Ma'am, I can't tell you anything. HIPAA laws are strictly enforced. But as soon as your friend welcomes guests, I'll let you know. You can wait here as long as you need."

"Thank you." She dug her phone out of her pocket. "I should try to call her husband again."

"I'm sorry. No cell phones in the hospital." She pointed to the sign on the wall with a cell phone in the middle of a red circle with a line through it.

Staci nodded slowly, shuffling toward the sliding front doors. But as she stared into the darkness, fear enveloped her. She was just going to step outside. She'd stay in a lighted area. It would all be fine.

Except the knot in her stomach suggested otherwise.

She huffed away the nerves and clenched her fists, praying for strength. She'd just walk out into the lighted area and make her call. Everything would be better when Tristan and Matt arrived.

Stepping into the inky night, she held her phone as though it were a lifeline, marching toward the sidewalk and stopping in the yellow beam of an overhead light.

It was just a quick phone call. She'd hurry to leave

Matt another message and be back before anyone could notice her.

"This is Matt. Leave a message."

"Matt, it's Staci Hayes again. Ashley's at—" She glanced at the sign over the E.R. entrance and read him the hospital's name. "They won't give me any information on her condition, but she's being cared for. Please, please call me back." After rattling off her number, she sighed and leaned against the wall.

Staring at her phone, she willed it to ring, to light up with Tristan's name. But he was gone. She was on her own.

But it couldn't hurt to leave him another message, too. His phone flipped straight to voice mail, but just the sound of his voice telling her he was sorry he'd missed her call wrapped around her, and she held on to it like a blanket around her shoulders.

"It's me. I'm at the hospital with Ashley. They won't give me any updates because I'm not family. But I'm here. And I…" She wanted to say she was sorry. She wanted to say that she was terrified.

Mostly she wanted to say that she loved him.

Even though it just begged to be broken, her heart knew the truth. She'd fallen in love with him. She wasn't what he needed, could never be what he wanted. But that didn't stop her heart from crying out for him.

"Well, I'll see you soon, I hope."

She hung up the phone, shaking her head and staring at the ground. Could she be any more absurd? Suddenly it seemed as if all the night's horrible events washed over her at once, sapping her energy and her courage. She wanted to be strong, to be brave…but she just couldn't anymore.

Instead, she hung her head and let the tears roll down her cheeks.

* * *

"Shh, Staci, it's okay."

Without a moment's hesitation, Tristan drew Staci into his arms and whispered the words into her ear. She jerked at his touch, her eyes filled with alarm for just an instant. Then she turned into his embrace, and he held her close. He murmured soothing words over and over. "It's okay. It's okay. Calm down. I'm here." He ran a hand over her curls and down the side of her face, stopping just before he reached the cut at the corner of her mouth.

Her hand fisted into the front of his T-shirt. Sobs burst out of her, followed quickly by a damp spot in the center of his chest.

He ran his hand in slow circles over her back as one of her arms snaked around his waist, her fingers twining into the belt loops of his khaki cargo shorts as if she wouldn't ever let him go.

"I was so scared."

"I know, sweetie." He had no idea what had scared her—the list of possibilities was long enough to span the globe. But at least she was talking.

"He came after us. And I never should have taken Ash—Ashley—" Suddenly she was fighting his embrace and pointing toward the hospital entrance. "She's in there. She was pushed down, and they won't tell me what's wrong."

"Shh. Calm down. Ashley's all right."

She looked up with watery eyes, her bottom lip trembling. "How do you know?"

With a thumb on each cheek, he brushed away her tears. "I was just inside. I parked at a different entrance, so I didn't see you until the desk nurse told me you had stepped outside. The training op was canceled, and when I got your voice mail, I came here right away. The nurse said Ashley was just coming out of surgery. She had a bit of bleeding, but they stopped it without trouble."

"And the baby?"

"They delivered him and he's perfect. They're taking good care of him in the neonatal ICU until Ashley's up to it."

"They are?" Long lashes blinked over her big green eyes, as though she couldn't believe him.

"Yes. They're both fine. Right now, I'm more worried about you. What happened?"

She threw her arms around him again, burrowing into his embrace. The tears were gone, but the knot in his stomach grew.

"It was horrible. He was right there, and he grabbed my arm, and I told Ashley to stay away, but she came after him. And he hit my face and I dropped the whistle. I tried to use it. I promise. But he was so big, and I couldn't see his face or his hair. And I kicked at him as hard as I could. I yelled for him to back off, but he didn't."

He held her just far enough away that he could look into her eyes, which were once again overflowing. His chest burned and his stomach rolled. "You did just what you were supposed to. I'm so proud of you."

She'd done everything she could. But he'd failed again. He'd failed to keep her safe, just like he had with Phoebe. He'd come so close to losing Staci. She'd become a staple in his life, and he'd almost lost her, too.

He knew he should pull away, knew that he'd proven that he wasn't good enough to keep her safe, but he couldn't stop himself from tugging her closer. Cautious of the cut at the corner of her mouth, he pressed his lips gently to hers. She sighed and fell against him, draping her arms over his shoulders and plunging her fingers into his hair.

The scent of hospital hand soap clung to her skin—the

sweetest smell he'd ever known. And as she deepened their connection, he held on to her. She wasn't an illusion or a figment of his dreams.

His pulse skittered in relief and exhilaration. She was safe and whole. He'd come close, but he hadn't lost her.

But could he hang on to her until the danger passed?

The lights of an approaching car blinded him, even through closed eyes, and he pulled back, leaving just one arm around her back. He couldn't tear his gaze from her battered face, regret a heavy stone in his gut. How long would he have to live with that?

"Maybe we should go back inside and see if we can see Ashley."

"I just want to try Matt one more time. I haven't heard back from him. Wait here with me?"

She nodded like he'd been a fool for asking as she sidled into the protection of his side, leaning her head on his shoulder.

The call must have gone straight to voice mail because several seconds later, he said, "Where are you, Rock? Get here. You're a dad, and you're missing it!"

When he pocketed the cell and guided her toward the entrance, she stopped before they reached the doors. "Why'd you call him Rock?" Her eyes were uncertain, her frown filled with questions.

"His last name is Waterstone, and he's built like a boulder. The rest of our class wasn't very creative when it came to nicknames." As they walked back inside and waited in the line to talk with the triage nurse again about Ashley's condition, he continued talking. "Now some of the guys are talking like they're going to call Ashley's little guy L.R."

"L.R.?"

"Little Rock. Like I'm Little—" He slammed on his mental brake. He'd never told her what L.T. stood for, and as her eyes grew wide, a half grin replacing the strain that had been etched into her features since he'd caught up to her, he knew he'd said too much.

She bit into her lip, her eyes all innocence and charm. "Like you're what, Tristan?"

"Nothing."

She wiggled against his side, one hand snaking around his waist, and he had to look away. "What exactly does L.T. stand for? You let me think it was short for *lieutenant,* but that's not the real truth, is it?"

He let out a groan, part humor, part very real pain. "No need to rehash this."

Her laughter, even at his expense, was better than the best orchestra playing "Ave Maria." "Did they call you Little Tristan?"

"There were two of us named Tristan, and the other guy was the size of Mount Rushmore. Obviously I was the smaller one. The instructors decided they needed to keep us straight, so they called him Big Tristan and me Little Tristan. The names just kind of stuck." He squeezed her until her giggle stopped. "I was the only Tristan in our class to make it through."

"I'm proud of you." She pressed onto her tiptoes and kissed his cheek.

Such a natural thing for a couple to do.

But they weren't a couple.

"Can I help you?" The nurse must have gone on her break, and the man in her place was about the same size as Big Tristan. His voice rattled the pens lining his perfectly organized desk.

"We'd like to see Ashley Waterstone."

"You related to her?"

"I'm her brother."

The lines around the man's mouth relaxed, as though

they were about to have words if Tristan claimed any other relationship to the patient. He consulted his computer and nodded slowly. "She's being transferred to recovery. You can head over in that direction." He pointed around a bend in the hallway. "Check in at the nurse's station. I don't have a room number for her yet."

"Thank you." Staci smiled at the behemoth, who responded with a genuine grin and a wink before putting his business face back on for the next person in line.

"I think if I'd been in line alone, I'd be stuck in the waiting room. You're some charmer, Hayes."

"See, I'm not completely useless."

Her words stopped him in midstride, and in the middle of the deserted hallway, he tilted up her chin until she had to look into his eyes. "Listen to me, Staci Hayes. Listen carefully. You're not useless. You've never been useless."

Head still tipped all the way back, she looked out of the corner of her eyes, avoiding contact with his, insecurities winding through the lines of her face. She didn't try to respond, so he grasped her shoulders in a solid yet gentle hold.

"You did everything that I trained you to do."

"Everything but the one thing I should have done. I should have stayed at the house and kept Ashley safe."

He stabbed a hand through his hair. "That's more my fault than yours. I should have told Ashley why she couldn't go anywhere. I could have saved all of us a lot of stress tonight."

Her gaze swung back to his, her chin quivering. "None of this would be happening if I hadn't found you and made you help me. This—what happened to Ashley is my fault."

"Hear me when I say this. You did the right thing. Without you, we wouldn't have known what was coming. We'd still be in the dark about what's been planned for Wednesday."

"But we don't really know anything, do we?"

How had he forgotten to tell her about his call with Salano? Of course, the scene in the entryway had distracted him. And that kiss still took up too many of his thoughts. "I talked to my FBI friend. He confirmed just what you suspected. Thanks to the tip we gave them, they've been able to work with other agencies to intercept some communications that point to the *Rockefeller* as the target of a bombing. And as far as they can tell, it's going to happen at the commissioning ceremony. Just like you figured." Her cheek was like silk beneath his thumb, and he smoothed it until her frown disappeared. "Our would-haves and should-haves aren't going to do a lot of good. We just have to be ready for Wednesday."

"Will they try to find him before then?"

"Yes. They're working every angle, but my team will be on the ground, and we'll do everything we need to do to protect the people at the base."

Her eyes lit up. "Can't you just cancel the ceremony? Then no one will be there. If no one's there, there won't be any injuries."

"I'm afraid it's not that simple. There are always people on the base—navy and civilians who work there. And if we foil the plan now, then we don't know when or where they'll strike again. Putting off the bombing isn't the goal here. Capturing the inside man and taking him out of the equation is."

"L.T.!"

He turned at the sound of his name as his best friend barreled down the hall. "Matt." He dropped his hands from Staci's shoulders to hug the other man, clapping him hard on the back.

"Got here fast as I could." His words came out on ragged breaths. "Ash? She okay?"

"We were just going to check on her and Little Rock." His swallow was followed by a quick gasp. "I'm a dad?"

FIFTEEN

Emotions still too close to the surface to be certain she could control them, Staci stood at the door of Ashley's hospital room. Leaning against the frame, she offered a wavering smile when Ashley looked up from the bundle of joy in her arms. Matt stood beside her, his arm around his wife and a hand over his son's little stocking cap.

Tristan stood just inside the door, his face nearly glowing.

"Come on, you two. Come look at him," Ashley said. "He's so handsome. Just like his daddy."

Matt looked like he'd never smiled so hard in his life, and Staci fought the tears burning the backs of her eyes. How could the sight of such a perfect family make her so sad? She just wanted to be happy for them, but the longing for and certainty that she'd never have a family of her own clawed at her heart. Here she was, an outsider among family, but they were waving her in, inviting her close.

Tristan stayed a step back, his eyes wide with wonder. "You did good, kid."

"She sure did." Matt kissed the top of his wife's head, and she closed her eyes, leaning into his embrace.

"I'm so tired," she sighed. "Having a baby is hard work."

"Well, you had a baby and emergency surgery at the

same time. You get a double pass. Why don't you close your eyes for a bit? We'll hold the baby."

After another loving look at her son, Ashley relinquished her hold on him, and the bundled baby disappeared into Matt's gentle embrace, the baby no bigger than part of Matt's arm.

"Come on, Staci. I bet if you ask nice, Matt will let you hold the little guy."

Staci shook her head quickly. "No. That's all right."

Matt held out his arms. "That would be great. I need to call Ashley's mom and let her know that little Jasper has arrived."

"Jasper?"

Matt glanced up from staring into the tiny face, eyes pinched closed and pink lips pursed and moving. "It was my foster dad's name. Thought he should carry it on." He nodded to the rocking chair next to the bed where Ashley had already fallen into the even breathing of restful sleep. "Want to sit down? I'll be gone just for a minute."

Her stomach clenched, torn between the desire to cradle the precious life to her chest and knowing that it would just further break her heart.

Tristan gave her a little nudge, and she slid into the chair. Before she could think about it, Matt leaned over her, slipping the bundle into her embrace. His little head fit into the crook of her arm, and his face broke, as if he was going to let out an ear-splitting scream. But he didn't. He just sighed and went back to making little sucking noises.

"You good?"

She nodded, never looking away from the precious child, even as Matt slipped from the room and Tristan pulled another chair up beside her. His big hand cupped Jasper's swaddled feet.

"He's so perfect." Jasper's feet kicked at the sound of Tristan's voice.

"I'm so glad." She sighed, letting herself at least enjoy the feeling of relief. "I was really worried. When we were there on the sidewalk, she said there was something wrong, but I didn't know what it was. And then the surgery—" A terrible thought crossed her mind. What if something had been injured that kept her from having another child? Staci didn't want company for her own misery.

She turned toward the sleeping woman, then back to Tristan, her voice low and scratchy. "Ashley wasn't permanently injured, was she?"

"What do you mean?"

"Um." She had to look away from the intensity of his gaze. "She'll be able to have more kids, right?"

"Sure. Why wouldn't she?" Confusion filled his eyes, but it was mixed with a tenderness that promised that he was trying to understand her question.

"Sometimes when things go wrong before a delivery and the mother has to go through surgery…" Despite the different situations, it was too close a reminder to her own situation. Heat rose up her cheeks, and she looked away. "Never mind."

He opened his mouth, as though he wanted to say more, to dig deeper. When he didn't, she sent him a smile filled with gratitude. She didn't want to have this conversation with him now.

Or ever.

They sat in silence for what felt like an hour but was probably closer to ten minutes. With each breathy sigh and gurgled grunt, Jasper stole another piece of her heart.

If only she could be part of his life, watch him grow into a young man. But that wasn't her role. She had no claim to this family.

She glanced at Tristan's face, his eyes alight with love, his mouth opening and closing as he mimed Jasper's movements. What wonders newborn babies wove on unsuspecting men.

If she had a right to Tristan's heart, maybe she could convince him to let her be a part of this family. But she didn't. Whatever was between them—a few kisses and an attraction that sent her blood pressure through the roof—had an expiration date. One way or another, their reason for being together would end in two days.

She'd be safe or—

Well, there was no need to think about the alternative.

No matter what, she'd be walking out of their lives on Wednesday.

Tristan's arm wrapped around her shoulders and he huddled over them. "You're a natural." His voice was smooth and thick like honey. "You're going to be a great mom some day."

The dam burst, tears gushing down her cheeks. She had to get out of there. "Take him," she cried, slipping Jasper into Tristan's waiting—if surprised—arms and running from the room.

Tristan couldn't sleep. He trudged through the kitchen, opening the fridge door, then closing it again. He filled up a glass with milk, downed half of it in one gulp and stared at the white liquid as though it could explain what was happening inside him.

But it didn't have any answers or rationalizations.

He set it on the counter, careful not to make enough noise to wake up Staci where she slept upstairs.

Just hours before she'd held his nephew and leaned into his embrace. Is that what it felt like to be a family? Like they belonged together?

He'd thought she'd felt it, too. But then she'd run away. He'd stopped himself from running after, reminding himself of all the reasons why they couldn't be together, couldn't build the family he'd craved in that moment when he'd had both Staci and that beautiful baby safe in his arms.

He'd tried that before. He'd tried to keep Phoebe safe. And that hadn't turned out well at all. Despite the promises he'd made to Staci that he'd keep her safe, he'd known they weren't guarantees, either—not for anything long-term. His job kept him away, would often leave her alone. There was just no way around it.

A footstep at the doorway jerked his attention to the figure shuffling into the kitchen. "Can't sleep, either?" Staci's words were low as she pulled her robe tighter over her leggings.

He held up his glass. "Just thirsty." Okay, that wasn't the whole truth, and based on her wry grin, she knew it.

"Want to talk about it?"

"About what?"

She pulled out an open pint of chocolate-covered cherry ice cream and grabbed a spoon from the drawer before settling into one of the stools across the counter from him. Scooping a spoonful of pink cream into her mouth, she sighed. "You have good ice cream."

"Thanks."

"I mean it. My sister only has that low-fat, low-sugar, low-taste stuff." She sighed, staring into the tub. "And try getting real ice cream in Lybania."

"You want a bowl for that?"

She shook her head. "Nope. I think I'll finish it off."

"What if I wanted some, too?" He didn't really, but her response would be telling.

"Get a spoon. And you'll have to hurry."

He laughed, shaking his head. "I guess I'll live without it."

She smiled. "Good. Now tell me what's going on."

He wasn't the one who'd broken down into tears when he'd paid her a compliment at the hospital. He had his stuff together. He knew what he was doing and trusted that they'd have everything in place to stop the man bent on destroying the new carrier and injuring hundreds. What he wanted to know was what was wrong with *her*. "I'm good. You?"

Staring into the bottom of her pint, she shrugged before digging out another scoop. "I'm okay."

"You sure? Because you looked kind of upset before at the hospital." He was walking on a rotting bridge. One misstep and he'd be in hot water. The problem was he couldn't tell which steps were the worst.

Her ears turned pink, a muscle in her neck jumping. "I've been thinking."

"About the ceremony and the attack?"

"No." She set down the spoon and scratched her neck. "I think it would be best for us to go our separate ways. After Wednesday, after he's captured... I know we haven't talked about this or anything, but I just think it would be better not to see each other again."

Her words were a kick to his shins, sharp pain exploding up his legs, and he sagged against the counter. Of course, they hadn't talked about what would happen after everything went down. He'd been focused on just getting through it.

This came out of left field, and he couldn't get his mind around it fast enough to respond.

"I don't understand." As he said the words, his stomach rolled, his head pounding with the reality. He tried to tell himself that this was for the best—that this was the smartest course of action for them to take, but for once, he couldn't make himself believe it. All he could think of was that this was the only girl he'd dared to think about a future with since Phoebe, and she didn't want any of it.

She blinked and licked her lips, still staring at the countertop and the empty carton next to her hand. He willed her to look into his eyes, to help him understand her words, but she didn't. "A clean break is best for both of us, I think. So let's just say our goodbyes now so it's not awkward later." She stood and walked toward the doorway, while he couldn't get his tongue to speak. Halfway into the darkness of the living room, she turned back, the tight lines around the corner of her mouth pained. "I appreciate everything you've done for me. I won't forget, and I'll always be grateful. But let's make fresh starts after this. All right?"

She didn't wait for him to agree. He wouldn't have.

Instead she turned and walked into the living room and up the stairs.

He leaned over the counter, resting his head in his hands. He felt like he'd just been run over by an inflatable boat.

He didn't want to lose her. But he didn't have a future to offer her, either.

Moving forward and sharing his life meant trusting that she would be okay when he couldn't be there. Because there would absolutely be days when he couldn't be at her side.

Could he trust that God would protect her when he couldn't?

On Wednesday morning, Staci awoke with a knot the size of the *Titanic* in her stomach. Whether it was from apprehension for the day ahead or the fact that she and Tristan hadn't said more than a dozen words to each other since she blurted out her thoughts two nights before, she didn't know.

The seasick feeling accompanying the knot suggested a combination of both was to blame. But somehow she could only focus on the latter.

She had been terrible. She had seen the confusion and hurt in his eyes, but in her rush to reestablish that barrier between them—the one she hoped would keep her from being hurt—she'd wounded him instead. That barrier from past rejection had made it safe for her to spend so much time with him. But it had vanished somewhere between the hours in the gym and a long slow kiss outside the hospital on the night of Jasper's birth.

She couldn't give him what he deserved—a family of his own. Despite her own attraction to him— Oh, who was she kidding? Despite that she'd fallen in love with him, she couldn't give him what he wanted. As sure as the tides rolled in from the ocean, she would be the one hurt when he lost interest in her after discovering the truth.

It had seemed so much easier to put up that blockade before the pain could go any deeper.

What a stupid plan. She'd meant to keep them both from thinking there was hope for more. But it was all she could dwell on now.

"God, help me to let him go." She whispered the words into her pillow just as a knock sounded on her door.

"We've got to roll in twenty. Be ready."

She pinched her eyes closed, knowing he was standing on the other side of the door waiting for her reply. "All right."

Immediately his boots clomped down the stairs, and she flipped back the covers, hurrying to get ready.

When they were in his truck and driving toward the base he finally addressed her. "You're going to stay with

Captain Earley's assistant today." Never taking his eyes off the road, he continued. "He's the commanding officer of the base, and he has a private office. We'll lock you inside until the whole thing's over. Got it?"

She nodded. "I guess. What will you do?"

"I'm going to find the man who sold out his country and tried to kill you, and then I'm going to make sure he never hurts anyone again."

He sounded calm and confident and she knew that she should find his words reassuring. But instead, all she felt was a new dose of dread. He was ready to wrap this up—ready to complete the mission.

Ready to say goodbye to her for good.

SIXTEEN

"Petty Officer Damaris Dominguez, I'd like you to meet Staci Hayes." Tristan pointed in Staci's direction, and the petty officer, second class, reached out to shake hands with her new ward.

"Nice to meet you, ma'am."

Dominguez didn't look old enough to have graduated college, let alone old enough to watch over his Staci. But there wasn't time to question his decision or second-guess the plan. Staci needed a safe place to stay, and the CO's office was as good as any on the base. Of course, the CO was seeing to his official responsibilities for the commissioning. He was schmoozing senators and other distinguished guests, so there should be no one to bother Staci and Dominguez. They could stay behind the locked door until he gave the all-clear.

Somehow that wasn't helping to soothe the pounding in his chest.

"You have your orders?" he asked. "No one but my team in or out of this office until we give the all-clear."

"Yes, sir."

He turned to Staci, whose eyes were marked by a shadow. "Will you be careful?" she asked.

"I'm always careful."

She smoothed the cotton of his shirt, her eyes never making it north of his collar. "I'm serious. We still don't know what's out there, or who's involved."

"We have every contingency plan in place." He cupped her cheek, desperate to push through the barrier that had separated them since the night of Jasper's birth. "There are Feds, agency and SEAL personnel swarming over this base. We won't let anyone get hurt."

Her smile wavered and she dropped her hands to her sides. He missed her touch immediately. "I'm not worried about just anyone. I'm— Well, just be careful. All right."

She'd been about to say that she was worried about him. He was sure of it.

That definitely didn't slow down his pulse. To do his job well, he had to leave her side. And that wasn't going to change on another mission. He was always going to have to leave. But it tore him open to even think of not having her to come back to each time. Could they make it work?

Taking a deep breath through his nose, he held on to her shoulders, keeping her at arm's length. "I'll be back. Just don't do anything crazy while I'm gone. All right?"

Her smile cut through him, and he had to physically hold himself back. If Dominguez had been anywhere else, he'd have hauled off and kissed her again. At least once.

Probably more than that.

He closed the door behind him before he thought about scrapping the whole operation, clearing the base and letting the ship sink.

But he hadn't invested years in training and service to the navy and his country to give up because of a girl. He wasn't that man.

Even if he did love her.

He'd just have to keep her safe long enough to make sure the base was secure and no one would ever threaten

Staci again. Then he'd tell her he didn't like her idea about fresh starts.

He didn't like it at all.

"You ready?" Matt fell into step beside him as he exited the administrative office building.

Tristan let out a long breath between tight lips. Any other op, and he'd have agreed wholeheartedly. But not this time. This was different. "How do you do it every time?"

Matt frowned and gave a small shake of his head. "What?"

"How do you leave Ashley—and now Jasper—at home every time you're on an operation? Doesn't that eat you up?"

"Man, you've got to realize that she's not yours to take care of anyway. Never was." Matt popped Tristan on the chest with the back of his hand. "We're not promised any moment beyond this one, no matter what our line of work or hers."

"Sure. I know. I just— Sometimes I wonder, what if I had been here?"

Matt stopped walking as they reached their rendezvous point, his head cocked to the side. "You talking about Phoebe?"

Tristan fit his earpiece and lip mic into place before responding. "Those carjackers targeted her because she was alone. If I'd been in town—"

"You would have done what? Refused to let her drive to and from work by herself, the same way she did all the time? You really think you could have changed the outcome of that day?"

Pain shot through his temple. He didn't like that question. "Maybe."

"Maybes'll kill your peace. You're either going to trust

that God will protect her or you'll drive yourself crazy. You're not in control."

"Is that how you make it through ops and deployments?"

Matt's eyes turned soft, and he was clearly thinking about Ashley. "You better believe that I'll do everything in my power to protect my wife and son. But what's not in my power is so much more than what is. You know that. You see it on every mission." He flicked his mic on and the rest of his words came through Tristan's earpiece. "You've got to trust her to someone who can handle that 'so much more.'"

Matt was right.

But could he do it? Could he give up the role of protector to the true Protector?

Willie G., Zig and River joined them, each wearing their BDUs and armed with minimal visible weapons. They clipped their earpieces into place, all performing a quick test of the equipment.

"All right, L.T. What's the plan?" Willie's shoulders shook as if he were eager to get to work.

"Rock and I are going to check on the carrier. We've got guards standing at every entrance, but we'll confirm that no one has entered or exited the ship today. Zig, Willie and River, you'll be scanning the crowd, mingling and keeping your eyes and ears open. The FBI says that the target is certainly the *Rockefeller,* so we're keeping the public far from it. But as far as the crowd knows, you all are basic MPs. Got it?"

"Yes, sir." Three voices in unison sounded through the bud in his ear.

"Keep your eyes open for anything out of the ordinary. And remember that he could be one of us."

"One of the five of us?" Willie's voice rose in surprise.

"No. You guys were all with me the whole day that we broke Staci out of that jail."

"Right."

River leaned forward, always the last to speak, but usually the most thoughtful. "What about the outside of the ship? What if an explosive was attached under the waterline? Wouldn't be visible, but it sure could do damage."

"Yes. Paisley's boat crew is in the water, checking for something like that." Tristan swallowed, forcing himself to say the rest. "But I have a feeling he'll want to put it in place himself to make sure nothing goes wrong. We know he has a trident tattoo and a good knowledge of the harbor, so if he isn't stationed here now, he probably was once. He'll know how to blend in with a crowd, just like you do. So go blend and look for someone who could be you.

"And if you see anything, radio it in. We've got FBI surveillance working the gate entrance and in the MPs office. Identify and subdue him. Easy as that. Any questions?"

"No, sir."

"All right. Let's do this. And Willie, try not to scare any kids."

Amidst Willie's blustering and the others' guffaws, they split, going to their assignments. Tristan took the lead as he and Matt jogged toward the enormous ship. At the gangway, he stopped to speak with the petty officer, third class, stationed on the pier. The young man snapped his salute, and Tristan quickly returned the gesture.

"Petty Officer Trainor, has anyone entered or exited the ship today?"

"Yes, sir."

Tristan's heart picked up speed. "Were you not given orders that no one was to enter or exit this vessel?"

The kid's eyes grew wide at the strained tone of Tristan's words. "Yes, sir. But the captain requested to come aboard.

He was delivering a package of personal items. He dropped it off just an hour ago."

He glanced at Matt, whose eyes reflected the same adrenaline rush. "Captain who?"

"Captain Crawford, the XO." The kid wasn't much over twenty, and his eyes swept back and forth nervously between the two SEALs. "He said he had permission, showed me his documentation."

Tristan's chest hurt, his lungs suddenly refusing to work. A dagger jabbed into his temple, and his ears rang, Crawford's face swimming before his eyes. His stomach rolled at the very idea that the base's XO could be a traitor. He had the respect of an entire naval base, and he'd thrown it away. For what?

Whatever the Lybanian terrorists had given him, it wouldn't be worth it when Tristan found him. He had stood right next to Crawford at the ball, chatting about Staci as if she were just another pretty girl.

Well, she wasn't just any pretty girl.

She was *his* pretty girl, and he wasn't about to let Crawford lay another hand on her.

There was no time to explain to the kid the error of his ways. Instead Tristan said, "Is he still on there? Or did he leave?"

"Yes, sir. He left, sir."

Tristan didn't wait for more, instead barreling past Trainor, Matt at his six.

At the top of the gangway, he motioned to Matt. "You like him for a bomb guy or is he just a delivery boy?"

Matt nodded. "If he left that pipe for Staci that you told me about, building the bombs himself is probably where he's most comfortable. He was an active SEAL, right?"

Tristan spoke into his mic. "Salano, you there?"

"Right here, L.T. What do you have?"

"Captain Crawford. I think he's our guy." Several men on the channel hissed in shock, although no one said anything. "Everyone keep your eyes out for him. Salano, can you check his background for me? I need to know his specialty. I'm guessing explosives and demo, but I need to know everything you've got."

"On it. Give us a few minutes."

"I'm not sure how much time we have." Tristan flipped off his mic. "You think it's got a timer?"

Matt shook his head as he took off running. "I have no idea. Until I see it, I won't know."

"If it were your device?"

"Yeah, I'd have a timer." He paused. "And I'd have a backup."

Blood roared through Tristan's ears, and he took a deep breath. He had to keep his head until they could find it. Push out everything but the facts in front of him.

At least he didn't have to worry about Staci's safety.

Matt paused on the deck, straight across from the six-story tower adorned with communication and radar antenna known as the island. It was the command center of the ship, the location of the bridge and the controls. Without it, the vessel was little more than a hunk of floating metal. "If his explosive was small enough to carry on, he's probably not trying to sink the ship. He's looking to seriously disable it and set off a fireworks show. Only one place to do that on a carrier."

Their boots thudded across the pristine flight deck as they raced into the narrow confines of the first floor, the flight deck control.

They ducked below every counter, peering into every crevice, hunting for the package that Crawford had delivered. Their flashlights did little in the cramped, windowless confines of the lowest level of the island.

The first two floors were empty, and even though they had the light through the windows to aid the search of the third level, they were still stumped. It wasn't until they reached the bridge—the level second from the top— that they found a telltale box. Right beneath the captain's leather chair.

"L.T., we found something on Crawford." Salano's voice came into his ear. "When he was an active SEAL twenty years ago, he was known for his creative explosive devices. Including nearly invisible trip wires. Watch yourself."

Staci tried again to start up a conversation with Damaris, but had no luck. She was sure that the other woman had some insight as to what was happening outside the confines of the office. She just wasn't sharing it. After pacing every wall, inspecting every plaque, Staci needed news from beyond.

"Did L.T. tell you when he would be in touch?"

"No, ma'am. I expect you'll know as soon as I do."

Staci cringed at the formal moniker. She wasn't a ma'am yet. She probably wasn't even much older than the petty officer. But the infuriatingly calm sailor kept her seat in one of the two plush chairs in front of the enormous oak desk.

"Do you have a way to connect with them? A radio signal we could listen to or something like that?"

"No, ma'am."

She wrung her hands, anything to keep them busy. Tristan could be anywhere out there, facing who knew what. What if he came face-to-face with the man she'd seen?

She wanted to pray for his safety. She wanted that sense of peace she knew came from heaven above. She wanted to wrap her arms around Tristan, knowing that she could be everything he ever wanted.

As regrets for the unchangeable past and fear for the uncertain present mixed, her hands began to shake, and she turned her back on Damaris, folding her hands and leaning against the wall next to the coat closet. *Oh, Lord, keep Tristan safe.* They were the only words that would form, and she repeated them over and over again.

Until three rapid thumps on the door jerked both women's attention to the door.

The knob unlocked, then turned and the captain with the salt-and-pepper hair that she'd met at the ball poked his head inside the room.

Damaris jumped to her feet and saluted the senior officer. "Sir."

He waved a quick salute that set Damaris back to normal and offered an apologetic smile. "Excuse me, ladies. Lieutenant Sawyer has been detained, but he'd like to speak with you, Petty Officer."

Apprehension fluttered in the pit of her stomach. Staci shot a questioning glance at Damaris, who also wore furrowed brows and a frown.

"I'm sorry, sir. Lieutenant Sawyer asked me to stay here until he returned. I'm not to leave her side."

"Oh." The captain frowned and looked at his watch. "Well, I suppose I could stay with her while you go see to L.T.'s request."

Staci pressed a hand over her quivering middle when he gave her a smooth grin. She shook her head at Damaris. Something was wrong. Tristan had said that he or someone from his team would come. And she'd barely met this man.

But Damaris's face had relaxed and she nodded. "All right. I'll be right back." She sailed out of the room, not even looking back when the captain closed and locked the door behind her. Staci noticed four angry scratches that marred the back of his hand. They were too wide to be from animal claws.

They looked more like they had come from human fingernails. *Her* fingernails.

Her eyes flew open, and she screamed as loud as her suddenly breathless lungs would allow. "Back off! Tristan is going to be here any minute."

She held up her fists like Tristan had showed her, making her stance as offensive and intimidating as she could. But the captain—Crawford—just smirked and strolled toward her as though she were as intimidating as a puppy.

She backed away until she hit the wall, her heart thudding painfully beneath her ribs. He just kept following her steps.

"Come now, Ms. Hayes. We're practically old friends at this point. No need to put up such defenses."

"You attacked me. You're trying to blow up the *Rockefeller*." She despised the weakness in her words. They were hardly more than a breath, and she gasped to replace the air they'd expelled.

He stepped toward her, and then set his hat down on the desk, smoothing down the sleeves of his white uniform, looking as if he were preparing for a casual walk across the base, not trying to sabotage the newest vessel in the U.S. Navy.

If he could be calm, maybe she could be, too. Tristan would come for her. She had no doubt. After all, he'd worked too hard to rescue her from this man and his cohorts once. Tristan wouldn't let them win the second go-around.

She just had to keep Crawford cool and talking until the SEAL Team FIFTEEN cavalry arrived.

Forcing her fists to her sides, she spread her fingers wide. "What do you want from me?"

Smacking his tongue, he shook his head. "It's not what I want from you. It's what you know that you shouldn't."

"Really?" She stepped into the corner of the desk, cringing as her hip bounced off it. "I don't think I know as much as you assume I do. I mean, I didn't even recognize your voice when we danced." Her skin crawled at the memory. She'd let him hold her hand and wrap an arm around her back.

"You know more than you let on. You know the faces of the men I met with. You took at least one piece of paper—a map, I think. And as long as you're around, you can always point the finger at me." He lunged toward her, and she scampered between the chairs, keeping as much furniture between them as possible. He was going to kill her. As sure as he stood across from her, he was going to get rid of her and any evidence he thought she had.

Fear began to work its ice-cold fingers through her brain once more, and she had to fight to form a response. "But—but I—I'm not the only one. Damaris knows that you're here with me. If you—" She couldn't say the words aloud. Squeezing her hands back into fists, she pressed on. "If something happens to me, she'll tell the authorities."

"And I'll tell them exactly what happened. When I turned my back, you ran, and no one has seen you since. Maybe you were less prisoner and more conspirator in Lybania."

"But there are security cameras and guards at the gate." She grasped for anything that might keep her sane, anything that would help her hang on to hope.

His sinister cackle filled the room so much louder than his following words. "It's good to be the XO."

He took three steps in her direction. She knew she should edge away, but paralysis had set in, her body numb, and she couldn't move.

"But why? Why give up your career and country?"

"You have no idea what kind of money and connections these people have." He leaned in enough that she could feel his breath and smell his cologne. "I can retire to a beach on Fiji if I want. What did the navy ever give me but a few scars and three divorces?"

Bile rose in her throat. Tristan wasn't going to make it in time, but she was not going to give in to Crawford without a fight.

Her breath hitched in her throat, his chest so close as he leered above her. What would Tristan say? Tell him to back off, push him away and run. Anything to escape. Just get free and get help. She didn't have to get far. Just outside. Then she could raise enough of a ruckus to attract help. Now was the time. He thought she was passive and wouldn't fight back.

He was wrong.

God, help me.

With all her might, she shoved her hands against his chest. He cursed and stumbled, but she had eyes only for the door, clawing at the locked knob. She almost had it undone when he grabbed her arm, wrenching her to the floor.

Her scream was part pain but more anger as she shot her fingers toward his eyes. Eyes. Groin. Shins. She repeated the words over and over, kicking and scratching.

Tristan had said not to waste her energy, but every movement kept him from easily pinning her down. Somehow, she knew if he had her fully pinned, she'd never get back up.

"L.T."

"I'm here."

"I've got a Petty Officer Dominguez here." Salano's voice crackled through his earpiece.

Tristan's stomach nosedived. "She's supposed to be with Staci. Where's Staci?"

"I don't know."

Before he consciously moved, he was running, flying down the gangway, nearly oblivious to the second set of bootsteps directly behind him. "Ask her. Ask Dominguez. Is Staci still in the CO's office?"

"Yes. Dominguez just left Staci there about two minutes ago."

He didn't need to ask who was with her. The pain in the very depth of his chest told him that Crawford had found his mark. Tristan had failed to protect her again. He hadn't been where she needed him to be, and he couldn't get there fast enough.

He had only one choice.

God, I can't protect her. Will You?

SEVENTEEN

"Let me go." Staci writhed under her attacker, twisting and turning to loosen his grip on her arm, but his fingers burrowed into the same place he had bruised her the night at Belmont Park. She cried out, and he slapped her face, again striking the spot still tender from their last brawl.

"Shut up." He swore, anger affecting his tone, and in that moment she recognized exactly the voice that she'd heard so many weeks before. Rage boiled in his eyes as he slammed her head against the floor, kneeling on her stomach. Stars flashed before her eyes for an instant. Dazed and starved for oxygen, she still flailed and fought him.

Just keep going until Tristan got back. She just had to keep going until then.

Her nails scraped at his face, and he yelped. Clawing like a cornered bobcat, she tried to suck in another breath only to choke on a sob she hadn't even known was there.

"Stop fighting. You're only making it hurt more."

"No."

The sound of a boot splintering the door frame accented her cry, and from the floor, she glanced over just as the heavy door swung in and Tristan thundered across the room, knocking Crawford to the floor and landing a punch that made her stomach roll.

Oh, sweet oxygen.

She could breathe again. Without the captain's weight pressing into her middle, she could finally grasp air.

Suddenly hands were on her, moving her to the wall. They didn't belong to Tristan, who was off to her left and had Crawford by the neck in a hold that would snap a smaller man in two. She swatted at the hands scooping her up, but a warm voice spoke in her ear.

"It's okay, ma'am. It's Willie."

She looked into the man's clear, calm eyes and rested her aching head against his shoulder. "Is Tristan all right?" The words sounded like they came from someone else, her voice was so husky and damaged.

"L.T.?" If Willie was surprised, he didn't hover on it. "Yes. He's fine. Crawford, on the other hand. He's going to be in a world of hurt when he wakes up."

"Wakes up?"

As he set her in one of the chairs, a second set of hands clasped hers. The entire room tilted, and she squeezed her eyes closed against the pain shooting along her temples.

"Staci? Can you hear me?"

She knew that voice and slumped toward it with a sigh. "Tristan."

Her eyelids suddenly weighed fifty pounds, and she fought to lift them enough to see his face. His lips were tight, his eyes narrow as he tucked her disheveled hair behind her ear. "Did you hit your head?"

She nodded slowly, stopping as soon as the fire lit up her scalp again. "Yes. On the back." Gentle fingers prodded the sore spot, and she jerked away from them.

"All right. You need to get to a hospital, right now. I can't come with you, but—"

His muscles turned tense, even the grip of his hand tightening. "You're sure? You got it?"

He didn't seem to be talking to her, but the way her head spun, she couldn't be sure of anything beyond her own name.

"And you checked to make sure there's not another one hidden somewhere else on the island?...Good man. I'm at the admin building with Staci. She needs an ambulance right away....Got it."

"Who—who are you talking to?"

He smoothed her hair down and gave her a soft smile. Years later, she could take out the memory of that smile and hold it close. She'd hang on to it forever, even if she couldn't hang on to him. "That was Matt. We got the bomb. It's all clear."

"Crawford?"

He glanced to a spot on the floor a few feet away. "When he comes to, he'll face a court marshal like he can't imagine."

"I'm sorry. I should have pushed him away harder." The thudding that circled her head called for a relief that only sleep could bring, and she let her eyes slide closed.

"You did great. You were incredible. Just stay with me, Hayes." He held her hand to his chest over the galloping motion of his heart. "Don't go to sleep. You hit your head pretty hard. Stay with me."

"You said that before." Clouded by sleep, her tongue stumbled on the words.

"When? Said what?" He paused for a long moment. Was she supposed to say something? "Staci?"

"In the jail. When you broke me out. Said I should stay with you." Her head lolled to the side, her neck no longer able to support its weight. "I did."

"Yes. You were great."

And then there were people everywhere in blue uniforms. Firm hands scooped her onto a flat bed, pressing a cushion around her neck until she couldn't move. And Tristan never let go of her hand.

"I have to stay here for now." He lifted her palm and kissed it gently.

Then she was gone, whisked out of the room and quite likely out of his life forever. He didn't need her anymore. The threat was gone.

And she couldn't give him what he wanted no matter how much she still needed him.

"The doctor said he'll discharge you in a couple hours when he comes through on rounds."

Staci rubbed one burning eye and tried to smile at the nurse. "Thank you." Her words barely a croak, she grabbed the plastic cup at her bedside table and sucked on the straw.

"Your head looks good, and your larynx is just bruised. It'll heal on its own. Just try not to use it too much."

She nodded, taking the admonition to heart. She didn't feel much like talking anyway. Not when the only thing waiting for her on the other side of the hospital doors was an empty house without the joy and noise that Tristan brought to it every day. Her life was going to feel doubly empty after sharing a roof with both him and Ashley for almost two weeks. But this was what she'd told him she wanted.

Maybe she'd start looking for a way to do aid work again. There were safer countries where she wouldn't be threatened by terrorists. There were lots of places in need of volunteers, in need of someone to care for children.

But none of those places had Tristan.

A shadow in the doorway caught her attention, and she swung toward it, her pulse picking up speed. When she recognized it was Tristan, her heart tripled its pace.

"Morning, Hayes. Up for a couple gentlemen visitors?"

He held out the perfectly bound blue bundle in his arms. "They let me take Jasper for a walk. You know uncles have a lot of responsibility when it comes to helping little guys become men."

"Lucky guy." Again, her words were little more than a croak, but she tried to paste on a grin wide enough to cover the joy and pain that warred in her chest. When every time she saw him could be her last, she couldn't find happiness in the moment. Why had he shown up, anyway? She'd said they needed a clean break. Maybe she should just give him a hint that it was all right to fall back. "I didn't expect to see you." *Again.*

He leaned a hip onto her mattress, crowding her space, and she pulled the lapels of her robe farther together over her hospital gown. He smelled of soap and spicy after-shave, which was wonderful after a night of inhaling only the cleaning fumes of the hospital.

"Where else was I going to be today?"

"I thought we agreed to make fresh starts."

As if she hadn't spoken, he continued. "I'm sorry I didn't make it in last night. By the time we had every-thing at the base cleaned up, the nurse wouldn't let me up to see you. She was harping on about visiting hours." He looked into Jasper's sweet face, a slow smile crawling across Tristan's mouth. "I thought about going stealth, but then I thought you might be resting, and I didn't want to wake you up after everything that happened yesterday."

His gaze lifted to meet hers, and a flicker of something unrecognizable lit in his eyes. "I had to stick around to see with my own eyes that Crawford was taken care of. He'll try for a plea bargain, but the JAG won't let him off the hook. He's going away for a long time, and he won't be able to ever hurt you again. I won't let him."

"Thank you." Her smile quivered under the pressure of

her shaking chin, and she pinched her eyes closed against the tears threatening to spill down her cheeks. Why did he have to say things like that? Things that made it sound as if he wanted to be part of her life? Taking a deep breath, she sighed its release. "It's okay. You're off the hook. You don't have to watch me anymore."

The corner of his mouth rose slowly. "I kind of like being on the hook when it comes to you."

Like a band around her heart had snapped, she grabbed her chest. If only that could be true. If only he knew the truth and could still feel that way.

Cradling his nephew in one arm, he reached out to run his fingers through her curls, which were probably a mess. Perfect. This would be his last memory of her, and she sounded like she'd swallowed a frog and probably looked like she'd been run over by a camel.

"Since Phoebe, I haven't really let a woman into my life. I tried with Robin, but I just couldn't let her in. It's why she eventually gave up on me. I just didn't think that I could live with myself if something happened to her while I was deployed. So I kept her, and every other woman, at bay, never letting anything get serious beyond a certain point. And then you showed up in my life."

She wanted to cling to his words, but she couldn't. Not when he didn't know the whole truth.

"And I wanted to be there for you, to protect you every step of the way. You were supposed to be just an extension of the mission, but all of a sudden you were the woman I couldn't wait to come home to at the end of the day. The woman who unapologetically stole my ice cream and faced down her worst fears to protect my sister. All of a sudden you were the woman I fell in—"

"No. D-don't say it." Her voice cracked, whether on a sob or just from the strain, she didn't know. It wasn't the only thing cracking, as the sound of her torn heart rang in her ears.

He shook his head slowly. The blue sapphire of his eyes shone in the fluorescent lights above, but he didn't look away. Two parallel lines formed between his eyebrows. "Why not?"

"I'm not what you think I am. I mean, I can't be enough." Tears finally broke free.

"What are you talking about? Tell me what's wrong."

She had to tell him now. If she waited, it would just hurt them both more later. And she loved him far too much to extend the pain. "You want a family, right?"

"I suppose." He licked his lips, the motion slow and thoughtful. "Haven't thought about it for a long time."

She looked up, not worried about hiding her tears. She needed to see his reaction, to brace herself for his rejection. "I'll never be able to have a baby. I can't give a husband children of his own."

Instead of leaning away, he leaned toward her, his ever-caressing thumb stroking the side of her cheek. And after a long pause, "I am so sorry. I can't imagine how hard that must be."

He wasn't leaving. What was wrong with him? "Did you hear me? You don't want me. I can't give you what you want. I'm not enough."

"Staci Hayes, listen to me. Whoever told you that lied to you. You are an incredible woman, tender and so strong. You survived a Middle Eastern prison and went toe-to-toe with Crawford. Most men couldn't do that."

A tiny bud of hope opened in her chest, but she pushed it aside. It would only hurt more when he changed his mind. "You don't want me?" She hadn't meant that to come out as a question. It was supposed to be a statement, telling him what was best. But now, she couldn't help but hold her breath as she waited for his answer.

"That's strange." His frown shook with an untold humor. "Because you're about all I've wanted since I met you. When you showed up in my trailer on the base, so petite and classy facing that hallway full of SEALs, I was already halfway to falling for you. No woman has ever done that before. You definitely impressed me.

"But I was so bound up in my past that I couldn't see to let that pain out or let anyone else in. Then you moved in, and it seemed like all I was doing was spilling my guts about Phoebe and my guilt."

She managed a watery smile. "Ashley did seem surprised that you had told me about her."

He moved a grunting Jasper from one arm to the other without looking down. "I should have known that she would tell you."

"She didn't want either of us to get hurt. She thought we were getting too close."

"Aren't we?" A wicked grin split his face, all white teeth and charm.

Oh, to be able to say yes. To be free to tell him that he'd never regret the choice to love her. But she could only shake her head.

Tristan shook his head, too, a mirror image. "Shake your head as much as you want, Hayes, but I'm not going away. It's taken me thirty-three years to meet someone like you." He swiped a thumb over the bruise on her cheek, catching a stray teardrop. "Look how hard you fought for me. You don't think I'd fight just as hard for you? I'm not going to blow this just because you're unsure."

"But I'm not." She clasped a hand over her mouth, her eyes widening. On a sigh, she said, "I just don't want you to have any regrets."

"The only thing I'd regret is not seeing what could happen between us. I'm betting you're a little bit in love with me." He cocked his head and arched an eyebrow, and she chewed on her lip before nodding slowly.

"You'll want a family."

"As far as I'm concerned you're more than enough family for me. You're so much more than I thought I'd have. If we get to the point where we want to add to our family, then we'll look into adoption. But for now, you're all I want."

And then the hope in her chest exploded and she couldn't hide it anymore. Careful of his special bundle, she threw her arms around his neck, and he pulled her close. Just a breath between their lips, she whispered, "Thank you for breaking me out of prison."

"Thank you for breaking me out of one, too."

EPILOGUE

Six months later

"Wheels up in thirty."

Tristan pulled his sunglasses off and glared at Willie G. "Don't you have something to do?" The junior SEAL laughed and turned back to pack the rest of his gear.

Staci reached up on her tiptoes, hanging on to Tristan's shoulders. "Give the kid a break. He's just jealous."

When she pressed her lips to his, he knew she was right. He wrapped an arm around her waist and leaned his forehead against hers.

"I'm going to miss you."

"I know." She laughed, her shoulders shaking and eyes dancing. Her ponytail swayed in the wind. "But it's only six months."

"Only six." Right. Six long months without her. But he'd face them in a heartbeat for the chance to come back home to six months like the ones they'd already shared together. He hadn't even realized how desolate his life had been until she'd come into it.

He didn't want to leave, didn't want to miss seeing her smile and tasting her lips every day. But it wasn't a crippling fear, just the ache of being away from the woman he loved.

"So six months," he repeated.

"Yep."

"That about long enough to plan a wedding?"

"Y—" Her voice broke off, and she dove into his shoulder, muffling the sound of her cries.

"Look at me, Hayes." She peeked up at him from under long lashes, a bashful smile playing across her glossy lips. That smile messed with his gut, leaving him a little breathless and far too stunned for the eloquent speech he'd planned. "You want to marry an old sailor who generally doesn't know when he'll be called away or for how long?"

"You make it sound so tempting." She squinted up at him, licking her lips as though in deep thought, and he squeezed her until she squealed. "Yes. Of course."

He kissed her long and slow, not at all concerned that they were outside the trailer of offices, in plain view of the rest of the base. She'd just agreed to be his and to let him be hers. Forever. No amount of catcalls or whistles would change that.

When she pulled away, her cheeks were flushed, he hoped by his kiss and the promise of their future together.

From the cargo pocket of his BDU pants, he pulled out a ring box and flipped it open toward her. She gasped as the sun's morning light caught the diamond surrounded by tiny emeralds. Touching it with a tentative finger, she glanced up as if asking if it was really for her.

He slipped it out of the case and reached for her hand. "It matches your eyes, and it reminded me of you." As he slid it into place, she didn't take her eyes off their linked hands until he said, "I love you, Staci Hayes. I'd go back to Lybania to rescue you any day you needed me."

"And I'd rescue you right back."

"And..."

She rubbed a finger over her new ring. "And I love you, too, Tristan Sawyer."

He had her back in his arms and nearly kissed when a whoop from the adjacent parking lot reached them. "Hey, now. We have young, impressionable eyes coming this way."

Tristan sighed and let Staci pull away as Matt and Ashley walked up. His navy bag slung over one shoulder and Jasper sitting on his other arm, Matt grinned a knowing smile. Staci held her left hand up to her cheek, and Ashley laughed and cried at the same time.

"He finally asked you?"

Staci nodded, her only response.

"Hey, what do you mean, 'finally'?"

Blond hair shaking about her face, Ashley only laughed at him before turning to Staci for quiet whispers and brilliant smiles.

"You coming, L.T.? Rock?"

Tristan glanced over his shoulder at Willie, hating that the kid was right. It was time to go. He pulled his fiancée close for one more kiss. Finally he had to pull back. "All right. I'll call you as soon as I can. Be careful." He meant it. He wanted her safe. But even when he was nearby, he couldn't protect her every moment. And he didn't have to. He just had to trust in the One who could.

"You take care of yourself, too. And Matt. Don't either one of you get shot. I don't need your casts or slings in my wedding pictures."

"*Your* wedding pictures?"

"Ours."

That gave him a lot to look forward to over the next few months. And it would be worth the wait.

* * * * *

Dear Reader,

I'm so glad that you joined Staci, Tristan and me on this exciting journey.

Have you ever met someone and instantly known that he was going to be an important part of your life? The first time I ever wrote about Tristan was in Matt and Ashley's book, *A Promise to Protect,* and I knew he was special. He's afraid of nothing except letting down the woman whom he loves. And it's left him in a prison just like the one he rescued Staci from.

Tristan's tale reminds me of the hope found in Isaiah 61:1. "The Lord hath anointed me to preach good tidings unto the meek; he hath sent me to bind up the broken-hearted, to proclaim liberty to the captives, and the opening of the prison to them that are bound."

Sometimes I'm tempted to let my fear keep me from the great things that God has planned for me. If you struggle with the same, I hope that you'll remember this verse. The good news of God's love offers healing for broken hearts and liberty for captives. We're set free. Just like Tristan and Staci.

Thanks for spending your time with us. I appreciate it more than I can express. And I'd love to hear from you. You can reach me at:

liz@lizjohnsonbooks.com
Twitter.com/LizJohnsonBooks
or Facebook.com/LizJohnsonBooks.

Questions for Discussion

1. Which character in this book do you most relate to? Why did you pick that person?

2. Staci is in the Middle East as a missionary. Have you ever been on the international mission field? What was your experience like?

3. If you've never been on a mission trip, to what country would you like to go? Why?

4. Some jail cells are physical and some we make for ourselves. Tristan lives in a prison of his own making, wrapped up in regrets from his past, wondering if he could have saved Phoebe. This keeps him from pursuing Staci. What regrets have you carried that kept you from pursuing good things God had in store for you?

5. Have you been able to let your regrets go or are you still carrying them? If you are still carrying them, what's keeping you from laying them down?

6. Because she is unable to have children, Staci struggles with feeling incomplete. Have you ever dealt with similar feelings? If you feel comfortable, share how you handled them.

7. What do you think it means to be whole? How do you know if you are or aren't?

8. Staci becomes good friends with Ashley and helps Ashley go through her pregnancy, the very thing Staci

wants but knows she'll never be able to have. Have you ever been in a similar position, watching a friend get the thing that you want? How did you react in that situation? Are you proud of what you did or would you change something about your actions?

9. Tristan must decide if he can trust God to protect the woman he loves. In what areas have you struggled to trust that God can protect or provide for you and your family?

10. The bonds of friendship in this story are important for Tristan and Matt and Staci and Ashley. What qualities do you think make these friendships so strong? What do you think is the most important criteria for a good friend?

11. One character chooses to give up his career and integrity and betray his country for wealth. How would you respond if given that choice?

12. Do you think Tristan and Staci are a good match for each other? Why or why not?

13. Do you think that Staci and Tristan will end up adding to their family by adopting a child?

Something clunked from the back of the bookstore, drawing Allison True's ever-vigilant attention. Her ears perking up, she rounded the end of the front counter. Another clunk sounded, and then another. Allison decided the noise was coming from the Kids' Korner, so she picked up the pace and veered toward the back right part of the store, creasing her brow.

She arrived in the area set up for kids. Her gaze zeroed in on a dark-haired toddler dressed in jeans and a red shirt, slowly yet methodically yanking books off a shelf, one after the other. Each book fell to the floor with a heavy clunk, and in between each sound, the little guy laughed, clearly enjoying the sound of his relatively harmless yet messy play.

Allison rushed over, noting there was no adult in sight. "Hey, there, bud," she said. "Whatcha doing?"

He turned big brown eyes fringed with long, dark eyelashes toward her. He looked vaguely familiar even though she was certain she'd never met this little boy.

"Fun!" A chubby hand sent another book crashing to the floor. He giggled and stomped his feet on the floor in a little happy dance. "See?"

Carefully she reached out and stilled his marauding hands. "Whoa, there, little guy." She gently pulled him away. "The books are supposed to stay on the shelf." Holding on to him, she cast her gaze about the enclosed area set aside for kids, but her view was limited by the tall bookshelves lined up from the edge of the Kids' Korner to the front of the store. "Are you here with your mommy or daddy?"

The boy tugged. "Daddy!" he squealed.

"Nicky!" a deep masculine voice replied behind her. "Oh, man. Looks like you've been making a mess."

A nebulous sense of familiarity swept through her at the sound of that voice. Not breathing, still holding the boy's hand, Allison slowly turned around. Her whole body froze and her heart gave a little spasm then fell to her toes as she looked into deep brown eyes that matched Nicky's.

Sam Franklin. The only man Allison had ever loved.

Pick up STORYBOOK ROMANCE
in October 2013 wherever Love Inspired® Books are sold.

LIEXP0913